CAPTAIN SATAN:
THE MASK OF THE DAMNED

CAPTAIN SATAN™
KING OF DETECTIVES

THE MASK OF
THE DAMNED

By William O'Sullivan

ALTUS PRESS • 2019

CHAPTER 1
FIFTY THOUSAND WITNESSES

JO DESHER, chief of the Federal Bureau of Investigation, blinked his eyes in the rays of the early October sun and glowered at the man in front of him.

"Are you listening, or aren't you?"

Cary Adair turned his face from the wide casement window that framed a view of New York Bay shimmering in the sunlight. Gray eyes, set in a smoothly rugged face that was tanned by the winds of seven seas, were lazily amused as they met the serious face of the F.B.I. chief.

"I haven't missed a word, Jo. Your complaint seems to be that you are in the F.B.I., and the F.B.I. has to work. Isn't that about the size of it?"

Desher heaved his stubby, powerful frame up out of the easy chair and looked helplessly around the luxurious room. "I know it sounds—unconvincing," he said. "Anything of the sort would, sitting in a room like this, with the sunlight streaming through the windows and the world of reality as far away as the North Pole."

Adair's teeth showed in a smile. He rubbed his strong chin with a browned hand. "Envious, Jo?"

Desher snorted. "I should say not! *I*—envy *you?* Hell, man— the only exercise you get is in clipping dividend coupons; and your only excitement is in finding new ways to spend them!"

Adair's face sobered suddenly. "Watching 'King Cal' Merrill pitch for the Titans in this World's Series will be—exciting,"

Hot lead poured into the weird, revealing light.

he murmured. "Which reminds me, we'll have to start soon if we want to see him warm up."

"If *you* want to see him warm up," Desher corrected him sourly. "I don't care if a game of baseball is never played again. What gets me is how the devil I let you talk me into coming up from Washington to go along with you! 'Something very important,' you tell me. And what do I find when I get here? A game between the Titans and the Sox!"

Cary Adair's face had nothing of humor in it now. He was sincerely impressive. "I always respected your powers of observation, Jo," he said. "Believe me when I say that it is important—to me!"

The F.B.I. chief studied Adair's face for a moment. His eyes dropped to the faultlessly tailored afternoon coat that draped Adair's broad shoulders. His gaze traveled down along the creases of the striped trousers to his white canvas spats.

"Okay, Cary," he sighed. He shook his head. "It's hard to believe that a chap like—" He seemed to catch himself, stopped.

Adair's face was bland. But there was a challenge in his eyes when Desher paused. "Come on, Jo. Say it! 'A chap like—'?"

Desher shrugged his meaty shoulders expressively. "Now, don't get sore, Cary. You've got to admit that you lead about the most useless existence of any man we know. What do you do, besides read or loll around your clubs or go to First Nights of new shows? Or—"

"Or haunt antique shops, and indulge my fancy for jade—and collect rare coins?" Adair finished the familiar jibe for him. "I—hunt; sometimes."

Desher's face cleared with the mirth that rocked him. "I've got to admit I'm wrong about you, Cary," he choked. "You hunt! That's your contribution to the world! You hunt!"

Desher wiped the tears of laughter from his eyes with a pocket handkerchief. He didn't see the new look that Adair had leveled on him, a glance that was half amused, half mocking. But he winced at the words that Adair dropped carelessly.

"I sometimes think the Federal Bureau of Investigation could use a good hunter," Adair observed drily. He avoided Desher's injured look and said without raising his voice:

"Jeremy!"

A door at the far end of the room swung on silent hinges. A tall, gangling man, whose severely black attire was as funereal as his long, sallow face, came quietly across the thick carpeting.

"Yes, Mr. Adair?"

"Two more highballs, Jeremy. Well iced. Hurry, or we'll be late for the game."

The man's sad, almost mournful eyes rested on Desher for a long moment. "Yes, sir," he murmured. He went soundlessly across the floor again.

"Highballs and baseball games," Desher muttered, his face twisted in an ironic smile. "Highballs and baseballs—when the government of the United States is drifting straight for the depths of—*something!*"

His eyes were far away, and his voice dropped to almost a whisper.

"There's a wreck ahead, Cary, just as surely as we're sitting here in your apartment. A wreck that only Satan could fathom. Or devise!"

The room darkened suddenly as the sun went behind a cloud. An almost electric air seemed to pervade the room. Adair was leaning forward in his chair, body tense and face stonily bleak. Deep lines of care were etched in Desher's face.

"Chaos!—Ruin!—War!—The dissolution of the United States," the head of the G-men said slowly, sibilantly, like a fortune teller reading a fearsome future through dead eyes and speaking with unwilling lips.

He gasped and whirled in his chair suddenly.

"Good Lord!"

ADAIR'S MANSERVANT stood tall and severely at Desher's elbow. His raised eyebrows were politely disapproving as he gazed down at him.

"I said, sir—your highball!"

"Oh!" Desher mopped his brow with a shaky hand. He laughed nervously. "You scared the very devil out of me, coming up that way." He was shamefaced as he downed most of the amber colored liquid at a gulp and watched Jeremy walk slowly away.

"Peculiar character, that," he nodded in the direction of the disappeared butler-valet.

"Jeremy?" Adair sipped his drink, then rocked his glass to and fro, his eyes on the tinkling ice. "I couldn't do without him. Valuable man."

"Yes," Desher said. But his eyes didn't seem to echo the agreement. "You've had him a long time, Cary, haven't you? Ever since I met you, and that's—let's see?—ten years."

"He's been with me longer than that," Adair smiled. "We've grown old together."

"How old?" Desher asked. He seemed to be trying to make the question casual.

Adair smiled broadly. "What would you guess?"

"Damn it, I don't know," the F.B.I. chief laughed heartily. "And I've never been able to find out. Can't even trap you into an admission!" His eyes were frankly studying Adair. "You could be anywhere between—thirty years old and fifty. Fifty-five, even!"

Adair laughed. "Oh, come off it, Jo! Fifty or fifty-five? You're not trying to get my goat, are you?"

Desher shrugged. "You know more history—and from a personal angle—than any man I ever knew. It takes time to get an intimate knowledge of the Boxer rebellion in China; of the Boer War—of the Spanish War—the World War; the history of Europe and the set-up in Soviet Russia; the—"

Adair held up a protesting hand. "As you've often pointed out, Jo, I haven't much else to do but read." He sipped his drink again. "You ready to start?"

The F.B.I. man drained his glass and stood. "Always changing the subject," he mourned. "Oh, well—"

Jeremy came out of his hiding and produced hats and coats. Adair took two tickets from his pocket and handed one to Desher. "Might get separated in the crowd, Jo. Better carry your own ticket."

The F.B.I. man put it away. Jeremy held his coat. He held Adair's coat, then handed the two their hats. While Adair was adjusting his derby on his sleekly-combed hair, Desher felt in his vest pocket for the bit of pasteboard.

"What the devil? Now, I could have sworn I stuck that ticket in this pocket!"

Jeremy stepped forward and stretched out a hand that seemed to be all long fingers. "In your hat, I believe, sir?"

"What?" Desher's eyes condemned the man of insanity. "In my hat?" He removed the headpiece and stared at it, then into it. His gaze was scornful when he turned it up to Jeremy's mournful eyes.

The gaunt servant merely stretched out an imperious hand and captured the headgear. His manner was one of boredom tinged with an infinite patience. He plucked the pasteboard from inside the hat and presented it to Desher.

"Your ticket, I believe?"

The Federal agent stared incredulously at the ticket, then at the hat. Adair bent a steady gaze on Jeremy.

"By any chance, do you remember where I put mine?"

The servant coughed. "On the table, sir. Next to the highball." He leaned over and picked it up. Adair stared at him for a short moment before he signed to Desher to precede him to the door. "Thank you, Jeremy," he said briefly before the door clicked shut.

"Not at all, sir," the servant murmured. "A pleasure, sir."

Downstairs, while they were waiting for Adair's chauffeur to pull up, Desher shook his head. "I guess this business is getting me down," he said. "I'm—goofy. Imagine my putting a ticket in my hat!"

Adair was thoughtful. "Yes," he said absently. Then, when they were in the sleek black limousine and rolling swiftly for the Canal Street ramp of the overhead highway that bordered New York's West Side, he spoke again,

"You mentioned that—that man, Satan," he reminded Desher. "You think he's actually mixed up in this business that has you bothered; this—er—problem of yours, whatever it is?"

A cloud came over Desher's face again. "I don't know," he murmured. "There's no real evidence of it. But if he didn't like the way things were shaping up in the United States—?" He shrugged expressively.

Adair's eyes were intent. "If he didn't like the way things were going," he pursued, "you think he might be the moving power behind this trouble?"

Desher nodded glumly. "I'm certain of it. The man is—incredible! Uncanny. A myth, almost."

Adair stared out the window at the vista of the Hudson River that unfolded north of Seventy-Second Street. He turned suddenly.

"Jo, you've fed me bits about this—this mystery man of yours. But I never gathered he was the type to wreck a country—*his own* country. I think you said he was an American," he added.

"That's what gets me," Desher admitted. "But—" He fell silent.

The car swerved off the highway into a cross street and sped east.

"Well," Adair said, his eyes quickening with interest as the ball park came into view, "you'll have dinner with me and tell me about it later. If you want to, that is. Meantime, here we are!"

"Yeah. Here we are," the F.B.I. man growled. "Here we are at a ball game when the country is slowly going screwy!"

Adair grinned; but there was an excitement in his manner that Desher caught and which made him look at his companion wonderingly.

"Keep your eyes open," Adair warned as they quit the car and merged with the slowly shuffling crowd that thronged the entrances. "There's something screwy, as you call it, about this game. I want to see if you notice what I did four days ago."

Desher was puzzled; but patient.

"Lead on, McDuff," he said ironically. "Nero fiddled while Rome burned. I guess I can watch a ball game while the U.S.A. goes for a ride down Niagara Falls!"

As they filed into Adair's field box between the home plate and first base, directly atop the Titan dugout, Adair waved greetings to a number of the players who were limbering up for the fourth game of the Series.

"Huh," Desher grunted. "Is there anyone you don't know, Cary?"

Adair's lips relaxed; but his eyes were intent on a tall, muscular man who was flinging a baseball to a burly catcher, farther down along the line of boxes. Desher's eyes followed his.

"That's King Cal, isn't it, Cary?"

Adair didn't seem to hear him, so deep was his preoccupation with the star hurler's delivery.

IT WAS midway through the game—in the beginning of the fifth inning—that things started to happen and Cary Adair's eyes showed tiny pin-points of excitement.

King Cal had retired the first man to face him, then came a

hit, a ringing single to deep right field. And then the famous hurler walked the next two men—*and a third!*

The ball park was in an uproar when the slugging hero of the Series came to bat. The Titan catcher turned and flashed an obvious signal to his manager. King Cal caught the sign and came in, his jaw jutting and his face a mask of rage.

The fans notched the bedlam up to a higher key. King Cal—the 'Human Ice Box'—madder than the greenest rookie at being yanked from the box! It was unbelievable!

Cary Adair turned an inquiring glance on Desher; but the federal man wasn't overly interested. "The best of 'em falter," he said in a bored voice. "This isn't the first time King Cal's been taken out of a game."

Adair's eyes were grimly amused. But he kept them glued to the field. King Cal was ranting at the catcher, and the manager was listening to the argument. The field captain of the team had joined the group, and the fans were going mad.

For the second time in the short series that would determine the championship of baseball, King Cal Merrill was being knocked out of the box—and showing a rage that was obviously understandable to the fans.

Desher turned to address a remark to Adair, but paused when he saw the coiled-spring tenseness of the man.

The catcher was walking over toward the dugout in an attempt to get away from the infuriated pitcher. Adair caught his eye and signaled. The big backstop came over.

"What's wrong with The King?" Adair asked him when he was close.

The catcher shook his head wearily. "Hell, I'm a catcher, not a mind reader. He was going fairly well for a couple of innings. But still—" The man paused and looked back over his shoulder at the group on the field. "It's got me, Mr. Adair. It's—*peculiar!*"

"I've been watching King Cal pitch for a long time," Adair said slowly, "and this series is the first time I've seen him lose his head and his composure." He was letting his eyes rove over the nearby crowd, taking in their frenzy.

Now, suddenly, he paused, his eyes on a box in the upper stands and directly overhead. Two men were leaning over the front of the enclosure and staring down at him. One, a square-faced, hard looking man with a dark fedora well down over his forehead, seemed particularly interested. The other was glancing away nervously at short intervals, then turning his eyes down on Adair and Desher and the catcher again.

All the others in the great stadium were intent on the small group that stood near the home plate.

The steady roar of the crowd rolled to a crashing yell. Adair turned. The Titan manager was pointing toward the far away dressing rooms. King Cal was going out of the game. And he didn't like it!

"Look," Adair called to the catcher. "Look at The King!"

The man had hurled his fielding mitt down on the ground and was kicking it viciously in front of him as he started for the showers.

Then, suddenly, Adair turned his eyes up to that box above him. Desher saw a strange light in his eyes and looked up also. The heavy-faced man above had made a quick, almost imperceptible motion with one of his hands—hands that were hanging down outside of the box.

A round, white object seemed to hang in midair for a moment, then fell toward the box in which Desher and Adair were sitting.

"He's dropping a baseball!" Desher exclaimed. "The crazy fool—" He put out his hands to catch the sphere.

But Adair was faster. With a shouted warning, he knocked Desher farther back into the box.

"*Down!*" he yelled, as he hurled himself away from the front of the box.

And then his voice was lost in the deafening explosion that followed.

A stunned silence fell over the crowd—until a high pitched scream of pain broke the spell. Adair scrambled to his feet with the acrid smell of burning powder strong in his nostrils.

The screaming continued, but was weaker. It came from the men in the box at Adair's right. The big catcher had disappeared, and Adair looked and saw him lying ominously still on the grass.

The whole incident seemed to etch itself in Adair's brain like a powerfully impressive picture. The man on the ground—the four badly injured fans in the box alongside—the curl of smoke that was rising from the floor of that box and disappearing into the clear October air—the gaping hole in the cement side of the boxes.

And King Cal Merrill walking slowly across the field—while a wave of players and police swept across the grounds toward the tragic scene.

Then Adair turned and looked up. The faces which had stared down from that box had disappeared. In their place were those of fans who had rushed forward to stare down at the stunning tragedy below.

Desher had climbed out of the box and was directing the police.

"…Two men in that upper box," he was saying. "I didn't get a particularly good look at them. But block all exits and search every man who leaves this place!"

"We'll be here all week, doing that!" one official exclaimed.

"I don't care if you're here all *year*," Desher barked. "Get going!"

Adair leaned over and motioned to Desher. "What do you make of it?"

"Make of it?" Desher's eyes were enraged. "Someone trying to get me, of course! What else? Pretty clever, too. Making a deadly bomb in the form of a baseball!"

Cary Adair's eyes were gently mocking. "Who else knew you were coming to this game? You didn't know it yourself, until you heard it from me when you got to New York!"

Desher's face was a study. "That's right," he said, his brows knitting in wonder. "Have you any reason to think that you—"

"Look," Adair cut in suddenly. "You *might* have been followed from Washington. What do you think?"

Desher nodded, his eyes alert. "That—trouble!"

"Exactly. Now, you haven't told me about it—*yet*. So I judge you want it covered up pretty well for the time being?"

"And how!" Desher growled. "If our suspicions ever got noised around, there'd be a financial crash the like of which has never been seen in this country! And a revolution, likely!"

"Well?" Adair's eyes were sober and steady on Desher. "Maybe you'll get those men, Jo. And maybe you're—er—not *ready* to get them yet. Do I make myself clear? There might be someone higher up—more important."

The F.B.I. man's eyes narrowed. "By God! You're right!" He turned swiftly and buttonholed a police inspector.

"McCall," he said, lowering his voice. "You handle this thing your own way. But keep me out of it! Tell the newsmen to keep my name out of it, too. Understand?"

The police official nodded. "Okay, Mr. Desher. But I'd like to get my hands on the murdering rat that did this!"

"I'm afraid your only chance is to try and trace the men through the tickets they held for those two seats." Desher turned, suddenly anxious to be out of the park. "Come on, Cary. Let's get out of this. I'm going to start my own investigation. But on the quiet!"

King Cal Merrill was mounting the steps of the clubhouse when Adair turned to follow Jo Desher out of the stands.

CHAPTER 2
THE MARK OF SATAN

B ACK AT Adair's penthouse apartment, Desher sat in deep silence. Adair was quietly relaxed in an easy chair, his eyes studying the Federal man. He seemed to be waiting for something.

At length the F.B.I. chief stirred. "What I can't figure out, Cary, is this: how, if those men didn't know I was at the ball park until they saw me, did they contrive to rig up a baseball bomb so quickly?"

Adair shrugged and lighted a cigarette before he answered. "What do you think?"

Desher pondered a moment more. "Is it possible that it was intended for someone else? And if so, for whom? And why was it aimed at our box?"

The clubman turned his head while he tossed the used match into the fireplace. His eyes were veiled when he faced Desher again. "Do you suppose a gambling ring was trying to put the Titan catcher out of commission? They say he's pretty badly hurt."

Desher snorted. "That's damned poor logic, Cary. Why, with the Titans losing the series, should any gambling ring try to cripple them? Now, if it were intended for one of the Sox players—had actually hurt a Sox star—" He opened his hands expressively.

"I can't fathom it," he finished hopelessly.

Adair exhaled a long puff of smoke and settled comfortably in his chair again. "How about telling me something of your—er—troubles in Washington, Jo?"

The F.B.I. man looked about him, in the manner of a man who is habitually on guard. When he spoke, it was with apparent reluctance.

"Cary," he said, his eyes troubled and his voice lowered. "The worst of this situation is that we don't know where to begin, and it seems next to impossible for us to avert a national catastrophe. However, I have a wild suspicion."

"Enlightening," Adair murmured.

"Well," Desher hesitated uneasily. "It's so far fetched, this notion of mine, that I'm almost ashamed to voice it. Yet I feel deep down in me that I'm on the right track."

Adair sat motionless, his eyes half closed and on the floor before him. Desher's words seemed to take form as they left his mouth, so still was the room. He seemed to take courage in that fact, seemed to be more sure of himself as he went on.

"It's fantastic, Cary. But not impossible. I've been working under cover, *and alone.* Not another man in the department is in my confidence on this. That's why—" He paused, his eyes studying the man in front of him. "That's why I've been so reluctant to tell even *you* about it."

Adair sat still, eyes unflickering, the smoke from his cigarette rising straight into the air in a thin column, like incense burning at the altar of some ancient Buddha. Desher drew in his breath slowly, filling his lungs like a swimmer about to plunge into the deep.

"Official Washington is slowly going crazy!" he said solemnly.

Adair moved with the shock of the thing, spilling cigarette

ashes to the carpet. His lips were smiling slightly when he murmured, "I know a lot of people who are in accord with you on that."

Desher was desperately serious. "Don't joke, Cary. This thing goes beyond any mere party lines, any selfish political thought. I have reason to know what I'm talking about."

"Well?"

Desher sat straight in his chair. "Cary, in the past three weeks, five startling things have happened. First, Secretary of the Navy Halding had ordered the merging of the Atlantic and Pacific fleets for a duty tour to the Philippine Islands. There's a Cabinet row on about it this very minute; has been, for ten days. President Kane is not in favor of it."

Adair squashed his cigarette out in the ash tray. "Coulter Kane is an able man. He can handle Halding."

Desher smiled grimly. "Can he? Halding is backed up in his demands by Secretary of War David Garlock. And that brings up item number two; Garlock wants the military force of the United States changed in such a way that the Army would lose eighty percent of its effectiveness in case of trouble."

"Just talk," Adair said. "War scare stuff." But he was attentive.

Desher shook his head. "I mean, *internal* trouble! Do you understand? Now, here's item three: the Treasury Department is thinking of trying a scheme that would break the value of the dollar to next to nothing—if it failed."

Adair's impatience was evident in his voice. "Go on, Jo. What are items four and five?"

"The Labor Department is letting things run haywire. They're thinking of permitting unionization of *all* Government employees!"

"All?"

"Including Army, Navy and Marines," Desher said grimly.

Adair gave a low whistle. "I see!"

"And item five? A certain Supreme Court Justice is—well—I think the man is mad!"

Desher paused, then asked: "And now can you see the picture?"

Adair shook his head. "No, Jo. It doesn't stand up. All President Coulter Kane has to do is demand the resignation of the cabinet members responsible. Then the whole thing is set right again."

"And that's just the point," Desher said, his face lined with care. "Rout the cabinet and what have you? Big Business is panicky enough now. A move like that would I bring about a financial crash that would make '29 look like nothing at all!"

"*Don't* do it and what have you?" Adair asked him.

Desher nodded slowly. "The same. Ruination—or worse!"

Adair's voice was grim.

"Revolution!"

ADAIR SPOKE after a brief silence. "But where does Satan come into this? You think that he—?" His pause invited a reply.

The F.B.I. man considered. "I don't know what to think," he said at last. "As I said before, if Satan—the *mythical* Captain Satan, if you prefer it—thought the present national set-up wasn't right and that a gang of boodlers were at work in Washington, he'd be capable of handling things in a damned strong and definite manner."

"Why?"

"Why? You mean, what's in it for him? He'd be setting things right and at the same time making a killing for himself."

"Robin Hood," Adair smiled. But his eyes were sober. "Robin Hood in the Twentieth Century!"

"All right," Desher waved a warning hand. "Laugh if you like, but I know the man!" He coughed slightly at Adair's quizzical look. "Well, I know him and I don't. I mean, I've met up with him; and I know that on the three occasions he beat us to the punch, we found our quarry stripped of whatever worldly goods they had possessed. *And* smashed as well."

"Sounds sensible," Adair offered. "Captain Satan is a private police force who gets his pay from the crooks instead of from the honest citizenry."

Desher grinned grudgingly. "That's about the size of it. I can't help but like the duffer. After all, he saved my life twice. Once, in Samoa, when we were running down a slave-trafficking gang, and the devils had caught me dead to rights. And once again when an international jewel smuggling gang had got the drop on me."

"That was eleven years ago," Adair mused. When Desher looked at him in astonishment, Adair explained: "It was the year before I met you, Jo."

Desher nodded. "He's an amazing man. Strong as an ox, cunning, daring. And as relentless as doom once he's on the track. But he's always signed himself in before. That's what makes me think I'm wrong in suspecting him."

"Signed himself in?" Adair frowned.

"Satan has a peculiar pride," Desher explained. "When he's in on a job, he lets us know. Let's *both* sides know, as a matter of fact. Whenever he strikes, he leaves behind him a mark. It's a silhouetted figure of Satan—horned head and pointed tail—with a pitchfork raised to attack."

"Spectacular," Adair murmured.

"A bit," Desher conceded. "But it strikes the fear of hell and of Satan himself to the hearts of the crooks he is hounding."

The clubman speculated. "But you have me puzzled, Jo. You say you think official Washington is slowly going crazy—or worse. Just who—?"

"Your guess is as good as mine," Desher said miserably. "I suspect that some gang is out to corner a fair share of our gold supply. Or to make a market killing. Or to wreck our present system and to set up a government of their own. Some terrifyingly big racketeers, at any rate. And to put over what I suspect they are trying, it would take plenty of hard cash in hand.

"I think—" he paused, his eyes pleading for belief and understanding. "I think that in some way, with some strange drug or other—by hypnosis, even, impossible as that sounds—that these officials I mentioned are being slowly changed in their natures. Their minds are being given a twist that makes them horrible menaces in their present positions!"

Adair's eyes were wide and fixed on Desher. "But, my God, Jo—?"

The F.B.I. man shrugged. "Fantastic, I agree. I have had the men shadowed; I have set guards on their kitchens, taken samples

21

of their food, even, for analysis. But I can't find anything suspicious. Still—"

He was silent for a moment, then spoke with solemn conviction. "Cary, it's just as if these men were themselves—and yet not themselves. Do you know what I mean?"

Adair was silent. The sun was sinking into the west and shadows were deepening in the corners of the room. But one shadow, longer and coming from the window across the room, seemed to *move* slightly. Adair sat forward and reached for a cigarette. Simultaneously, a low buzz sounded from the corner where the pantry door was located.

"A few lights and a highball would be in order," Adair said casually. "I feel... chilly."

"Sounds good to—"

A loud explosion sounded on the roof outside, drowning out the F.B.I. chief's words. And on the echoes of it came another explosion, and the tinkling of glass.

A whistling missile split the air of the room and *thucked* into the panelled wall.

"Down!" Desher yelled as he dived for the table and rolled under it. "We're being fired at!"

The pantry door opened and Jeremy came swiftly across the room, setting his tray of glasses on the table as he passed. Something was at the window—a shadowy form that reached a hand for support against the closed casement, then sank slowly to the tiled terrace.

Jeremy jerked the window open. Desher ranged at his side,

drawn gun leveled, "Get away, you fool!" he snapped. "Do you want to be killed?"

Adair signed Jeremy to back away. They watched Desher peer cautiously out on the terrace. He stood rooted in his tracks, his eyes staring and unbelieving.

"It's—it's Eastham," he stammered. "One of my new men!"

He was raising his foot to step out onto the terrace. But he halted suddenly, his face draining of color slowly.

"Look!" His voice was hoarse with emotion and shock. "Cary—*look!*"

There, on the multi-colored tiles of the terrace, was a device cut out of some material like black felt—a round, horned head with a hooked nose, and a clawed hand holding a tined pitchfork aloft.

"Captain Satan is back!"

CHAPTER 3
THE AMBASSADORS
FROM HELL

CARY ADAIR and Jeremy stood clear of the agents who milled through the room a half hour later—photographing, checking, measuring, examining, reporting back to their chief.

Jo Desher, his face grave but drawn, gave a few last orders and dismissed the men. He sank into a chair when the last of them had departed.

"I don't have to tell you that you're to keep this to yourself?" His eyes were on Adair, then shifted to the servant.

"We shall," Adair assured him grimly. "There's altogether too much excitement going around here right now. First, we're bombed. Then one of your own men tries to take a pot shot at you through my window."

Desher shook his head. "I can't credit it. Eastham was new, of course. But we check our men pretty thoroughly, Cary. We're *re*checking on Eastham right now. What gets me is *how* in God's name Satan got up here to shoot him; *why* he shot him—and *where* he disappeared to?" His eyes shifted to Jeremy. "You certainly came out of that pantry as though the devil himself were on your tail."

The gaunt servant nodded in melancholy remembrance. "When the buzzer sounded, I started getting the highballs ready. Then came that shot. So I ran through here and—"

"Yes, yes; we know all that." The F.B.I. man stared at the gaunt man a moment. "How long does it take to make two highballs, Jeremy?"

The servant considered. "Iced? I should say that, normally, good time would be perhaps—" he nodded confidently—"a few minutes."

Desher grunted. " 'A few minutes!' Very accurate, that. Well, you made them quickly enough, didn't you? I was just thinking that—" He fell silent, his eyes calculating. Adair grinned.

"Jeremy?" he said with mock severity. "Are you by any chance Mr. Desher's friend, Satan?"

The man shook his head somberly. "I can't say that I am, sir; but I do feel like the Devil about this awful mess on the terrace!"

Adair chuckled. Desher's face relaxed into a grudging grin. "I don't think we'll arrest you yet, Jeremy. Especially if you mix me another of your highball specials. I need it." He fell silent again, staring morosely into the soft light cast by a lamp on the table.

Only about twenty seconds had passed when the pantry door swung open again and Jeremy started into the room. Adair whirled.

"*Fresh* highballs!" he said coldly. Then, with an edge to his voice: "*What are you thinking of, Jeremy?*"

Jo Desher

25

The butler-valet was sliding behind the door when Desher looked up.

"Eh?" the F.B.I. man said absently. "What's that, Cary?"

"I was merely reprimanding Jeremy," Adair told him. "Something I seldom have to do." He added after a moment: "Fortunately for Jeremy!"

Desher stared. "You're a queer one, Cary. You loll around doing nothing and just laughing away your time. Yet you can be severe about the smallest things."

Adair walked to the window and stood looking down at the harbor lights on the bay. "Small things," he said, "are important."

Desher shrugged. "Can you come to Washington with me, Cary? I'd like to talk this thing over with my chief—the head of the Department of Justice? Maybe he'll want to ask a few questions."

Adair made a grimace of distaste. "You know me, Jo. I hate any—er—official business of this kind. And besides, you saw more of it than I did. I'm afraid I can't help you, old man. Frankly, I have made up my mind already to take some time off—to get away from all this. I don't like it; right at my own doorsteps."

The F.B.I. agent shook his head. "You're a help!" But his eyes weren't accusing, if his voice was. They were more curious. "What do you plan to do? Where are you going?"

"Oh," Adair yawned, "I think a little hunting will divert me. I feel rusty. Need my wits and my eye sharpened up a bit."

"Hunting," Desher grunted derisively. "Hunting, while I'm going after the biggest game in the world—Captain Satan!"

Adair smiled. "You and your Captain Satan! But at any rate, you've decided he's your man, that he's behind all this? And guilty of killing Eastham as well!"

"Who else?" Desher asked. "You saw the evidence yourself."

"I saw that Eastham was about to fire into this room," Adair said calmly. *"Did* fire into it, as a matter of fact. His aim was spoiled by—whoever killed him."

"Satan's the man to follow," Desher said doggedly. "If he isn't the man behind all this, then he's *after* the men who are! So, all the more reason for following him. I may get both Satan and his prey."

Jeremy entered with the drinks and set them on the table. Desher stood and walked uncertainly down the room. "Your washroom is down this way, isn't it, Cary?" he was asking.

But before he got an answer he had pushed open the pantry door and stood stock still, staring ahead of him with widening eyes.

"What are all these drinks on the serving table?"

Adair walked over slowly, saying, "The washroom's on this side, Jo." And as he did, Jeremy slipped past Desher and into the serving pantry.

Desher's eyes were narrowed. "I asked you what all these drinks were doing here?" he repeated steadily. "Do you keep highball set-ups ready by the dozen?"

Jeremy's suave voice interrupted. "If you'll excuse me, sir—*two* drinks are here; not a dozen. They are the ones I had mixed at the time of the—er—shooting. Mr. Adair ordered fresh ones."

"Two?" Desher's voice was heavy with scorn. "Do you think

I'm crazy? There's something decidedly funny about—" His voice faltered, then went dead. His eyes were on the serving stand—where there were *two* tall, amber colored goblets, filled to brimming. Not another object was on the table. Desher's hand went to his head.

"I—I guess I'm tired out," he muttered as he made his way to the washroom at the other side.

Jeremy avoided Cary Adair's eyes.

THE F.B.I. man returned to make several routine telephone calls. When he was through with them, he prepared to make his departure.

"Well," Desher said sourly, "I owe you a vote of thanks for saving me from catching that baseball bomb to-day." His eyes were faintly puzzled as he spoke. "Sorry you can't see this thing as important enough to come to Washington and—" He broke off suddenly, was following another train of thought.

"What made you stop me from catching that baseball—that bomb?"

Adair smiled. "Call it a hunch. Call it sheer luck. But anyway, Jo, if it had been just what it seemed—a baseball and nothing more—I shouldn't have ventured catching it. Might have broken your hands. Accidents will happen, you know."

Desher guffawed, his face clearing. "You're as soft as the life you lead." In a moment he pulled his automatic from his pocket and examined it carefully as he prepared to go. "Just in case," he was saying grimly.

Jeremy, holding his coat, coughed discreetly. Desher returned the gun to his pocket and let the servant help him into his coat.

Jeremy brushed lapels and collar with a solicitous hand, then passed the Federal man his hat.

"You're tired, old man," Adair murmured, guiding Desher to the door with a hand on his elbow. "A night's sleep will fix you. Nice of you to come up, Jo. I appreciate it, despite this mess."

"Oh!" Desher halted. "What was it you wanted of me, Cary? Something about the ball game, as I recall?"

Adair's face was blandly innocent. "You have marvelous powers of observation, Jo. I wondered—who do you think will win the Series?"

"Great God!" Desher exclaimed, his eyes wide. "You brought me all the way up here to—? Good night!" He slammed the door after him.

Adair turned to Jeremy. "You heard? About the hunting trip?"

"Yes, sir. The—ah—guides are being notified."

"Good." Adair smiled slightly. "You have the 'permit'? I think I saw you—?"

"Oh, I hope not, sir," Jeremy murmured. "Not *saw* me, sir?" He sighed. "It's a long time, sir, since I've had any real practice. A sleight-of-hand artist should never let his hand lose its touch, should he, sir!"

"I noticed you were thinking of that earlier to-day," Adair said with gentle irony. "In your place, I should reserve my practice until it proved more profitable, Jeremy!"

Jeremy's hand went to his coat pocket. He extracted a flat, black wallet which he opened to display a half-dozen bills of large denomination.

"I found it quite profitable to-day, sir," he observed mildly.

29

Adair's face split in a broad grin. "Give me my wallet, you ass! Now, get to the packing. You know which clothes." He paused, counting his orders off on his fingers. "Money. Plenty of it, too. Let the apartment manager know we shall be away indefinitely, let us say. Guns, of course. You have them?"

"I have two more than usual, sir. Recently acquired."

Adair stood in contemplation for some minutes, his eyes on the wall. When he turned to Jeremy again, there was a lazy excitement in his manner.

"Two highballs, Jeremy." He smiled meaningly: "They needn't be fresh ones!"

The servant was back in ten seconds, a glass in either hand. Solemnly, they raised the goblets in a toast, eyes sober and steady. Adair grinned and said slowly:

"Happy hunting, Jeremy!"

"Happy hunting—" the butler-valet paused imperceptibly. "Sir," he added.

THE INKY blackness of Pier Four was split by a fugitive ray of light, then was plunged into darkness again so quickly that it was as if a giant lightning bug had flown along the dank, dark place, lighted once, then gone on.

A low whistle sounded from the darkness, and in its wake came a blinding flash of light, which stayed on, this time.

There was a gasp when the strong beam outlined clearly a group of men standing close to one corner—a gasp that was evoked by the silhouetted figure of a rampant Satan, thrown on the wall above them.

"Silence!" Although the command was scarcely more than a

whisper, it had the crack of a whiplash. Then: "Who made that noise?"

There was an uneasy stirring and a murmur of denials from the assembled men. "Skip it. Shut up," came that harsh, low voice again. "Slim!"

"Right, Captain?"

A tall, spare man with a sad but intelligent face stood forward from one side of the covered wharf. The ray of light stabbed at him, bringing into clear view the man's steady brown eyes, his calm, strong mouth.

"All present?"

"All that are coming," the man addressed as Slim answered. "Dutch and Paddy are—gone." He stepped forward. A hand with long, sensitive fingers held out a sheaf of papers. "Here's the dope sheets."

"Good!" The figure with the light held the papers slightly in front of him, managing to keep out of the spot of light himself. His voice was terse. "Roll call, men. Answer your name quickly and softly." He paused.

"Happy?"

"Here, Cap'n."

The strong light shifted to the man who stepped forward. Short, he was, stocky, with merry blue eyes that would be darker in a less powerful light; a face that was round and dimpled in a smile as he stared steadily back into the beam.

"Glad to see you, Happy. How's the Missus and the kids?"

"Swell, Cap'n. It's good to be back with you."

The voice that came from behind that beam was slow and

serious. "Let's hope you'll feel that way when we're through! Sledge?"

"Here."

There was a momentary silence. Then: *"What?"*

The light played on a big, powerfully built man with a broken nose and scarred face. Small black eyes squinted almost shut against the beam that focused on them unmercifully.

"Here—Captain Satan," the voice of the man answering to 'Sledge' tried.

There was a sudden stir among the others. The voice behind the beam was icy when it spoke again. "You've… changed somewhat, Sledge. That scar is a bit newer than I remember it."

The other was silent a long moment. Then: "It's—it's been a long time, Captain. Three years, I guess."

The forms around the big man seemed to melt away into the darkness, leaving him alone. He stirred uneasily, was looking around when that voice stopped him.

"You fool!" A hard, short laugh jarred him back a step. "Every year Satan's Crew gets together for a week—work or no work. Did you think we'd rust for three years and then come into the field again?"

The big man edged to one side a bit. But the beam followed him inexorably. "I meant, eleven years since we worked a real job, Captain," the man whined. "I didn't mean—"

"No man of mine calls me 'Captain,' except one. That's Slim!"

"I forgot—"

The voice crushed his words back again. "No man of mine shuts his eyes when this ray hits them!"

The big man tensed but stood silent.

"Slim!"

"Right, Captain?" the response came.

A strong, brown hand shoved a paper into the beam. "Here's Sledge's dope sheet. Check this man's fingerprints with those on his sheet. Ask him the questions, first! The questions that are on there!"

The tall man took the paper and turned. "Age?"

"Thirty-five."

"Your call letters, in case of emergency?"

Silence. Silence that was tinged with something electric as the big man's chest rose and fell with hard breathing.

"Fingerprints, Slim."

"Right, Capt—"

The man at bay went into action with the speed of light. His right hand whipped to the lapel of his coat—but never quite reached it. A streak of orange flame licked through the dark, merged with that hard beam of light, punched on to knock the big man back three paces. But there was no more sound to it than to a short, sharp cough.

THREE PAIRS of arms shot into the spot of light and lowered the sagging frame of the big man to the floor.

"I hope that's all of *that*," the voice behind the light said meaningly. The rest of the roll call went uninterrupted.

"Doc." A bronzed little man with capable hands and keen gray eyes stepped forward.

"Got your tools with you, Doc? Better take a look at that four-flusher and see if there's any life left in him."

Captain Satan is back!

The man called Doc produced a stethoscope and used it briefly. "You still shoot straight, Cap'n," he said dryly when he straightened.

"Frenchy!" A slim, good looking man with a debonair mustache and glittering black eyes stepped forward.

"Soapy!" A short, slinky, nondescript man. "Gentleman Dan!" Tall, graceful, blond, wearing a quiet smile. "Kayo!" A thick-set chap with the meaty shoulders and huge frame of a wrestler. "Big Bill!" A seedy looking, shuffling, oversized man with bleary eyes and a toothless grin. But his voice was soft and grave.

"*How* are you, Cap'n?"

The voice behind the beam chuckled. "Darned if you don't look drunk even now, Bill!"

"And I still can't stomach three drinks of the stuff," Big Bill said wearily.

"Valuable man! Mike?"

"Yes, Cap'n, sorr," a rich brogue answered. Mike showed himself in the light to be a portly individual with earnest eyes that managed to be serio-comic. Red hair thatched a perfectly round head, and a wispy, reddish mustache drooped despondently at the corners of a strong, wide mouth.

The brown hand thrust the papers into the beam again. "Never mind checking any other prints, Slim. I knew my men!"

"Thank you, Cap'n," a number of voices chorused softly.

"Now—for this renegade. In some ways he looked enough like Sledge to pretty near fool me. I'm satisfied that the real Sledge is gone, men. Otherwise this man wouldn't have dared try this stunt. What do you think, Gentleman Dan?"

"Right as rain, Cap'n," the tall one drawled. "I'd say he did Sledge in, myself."

The voice behind the light was suddenly harsh. "Cut a strip of his coat—take one shoe—see if he has any laundry marks on his shirt, underwear or socks. Gentleman Dan will check them, try to trace them. I want to know who this man is. *Was,* rather! And I don't want any bungling. It's important!"

"I'll get the dope, Cap'n," Gentleman Dan said quietly.

"That's the spirit! Now—Slim? You have the canvas cover? You'd better stretch it across that far corner." The light stabbed in the direction which was meant. "Be sure no crack is left in it to let any light through!"

"Right, Captain."

In the rays of the beam, a canvas, braced by folding steel uprights no stouter than a pencil, formed a small tent. Quietly and quickly the men filed under its cover. The beam of light saw them in, then followed slowly after the last one.

The cleverly contrived den of canvas was lighted bright as day by the strong lamp, and the Mark of Satan stood large and forbidding on a side of it as the men sank to sitting positions on the floor.

Then the flap dropped and the wharf was plunged into darkness again—a darkness that held the corpse of the man who had failed to fool Satan.

CHAPTER 4
SATAN'S SWEEPSTAKES

WHEN THE flap of the improvised tent had dropped to enfold the group, the voice behind that lamp became the figure of a man. The lamp was set on the floor where it threw a halo of light over the men who sat cross-legged there.

Captain Satan remained standing.

His tight fitting black coat was buttoned over a black sweater, showing the perfect symmetry and powerful muscles of the man. Black trousers and rubber-soled black shoes completed a garb that would blend with the unlighted night outside the wharf.

But it was Satan's face that attracted all eyes there.

Square without being heavy, with a strong, well rounded chin, ears ample and flat against the head—a head that was cropped as close as a convict's. Stern gray eyes were framed in a face that was brown as an Indian's. The nose was straight.

Satan moved, his sloping shoulders and large biceps speaking of the tremendous power of the man. But it was the sort of power that could be effectively and deceptively concealed had he chosen to wear looser fitting clothes.

His straight, strong mouth was clamped tight for a moment while he let his eyes range over his men. In the shadows behind him, standing in the half-gloom where the light didn't touch, stood Satan's assistant and right hand man, Slim. Without turning, Satan spoke to him.

"Everybody here on time, Slim?"

"Soapy was late, Captain," Slim said quietly. "Thirty minutes."

The gray eyes shifted to the nondescript little man in front of him. "Well, Soapy?"

"I wuz at the ball game, Cap'n. There was an explosion an'—"

"I know that," Satan said harshly. "But why were you late?"

"Gee, Cap'n—when that terrific *wham* came—y'see, I wuz in th' upper stands, right over where it happened. I seen that big G-man, Desher, an' some dude who was with him. I seen it must a' been for Desher. The dude took a dive. Well, I—"

"Get to the point!"

Soapy's nervousness vanished behind a resigned calm. "Right, Cap'n. I followed two guys I seen take it on the lam. They wuz sittin' in a box right over where it happened."

Satan's eyes narrowed. "Where did you follow them to?"

"They shot away from the ball park in a big, black car. I hitched on the tail of it till we wuz clear o' heavy traffic, an' then I hopped a taxi an' tailed them the rest o' the way in that. They went to the Atlas Bank n' Trust's main branch."

"And came right out again?"

"Naw. I seen 'em go through a gate marked private an' disappear into the offices. The special cops on duty give 'em the salute, so I figgered they wuz—"

"Why did you follow them?"

The question was rapped out like the blows of a riveting machine. Soapy swallowed audibly. "It wuzn't a shakedown, Cap'n. Honest it wuzn't! It wuz jist a funny hunch I had. I says to meself, I says, 'Soapy, you better tag these guys—'"

Satan's strong face was relieved by a smile that showed even, strong teeth. His eyes glinted. "All right, Soapy. I believe you. But that was early yesterday afternoon, wasn't it? It's now three in the morning. *Why were you late?*"

"I waited right outside the Atlas Bank, Cap'n. Them guys didn't come out again. I guess they're still there."

"Then how'd you hear about this meeting?"

"Luck, Cap'n. Gentleman Dan came walkin' down Broadway, an' he seen me. He give me the office to lam over here."

"But you waited! That right?"

Soapy's eyes fell. "That's right, Cap'n," he said after a moment.

Satan turned to Slim. "Fine Soapy a thousand dollars, Slim—when and if we collect on our present job." His eyes went to the tall, blond man. "You heard, Gentleman Dan? Soapy telling the truth?"

"Quite, Cap'n." Gentleman Dan turned his attention to his fingernails. Satan's eyes ranged over his crew.

"I want you all to listen carefully," he told them. "We're after the biggest game of our lives, men. But if we slip, it won't be funny, it won't be any game. *It'll be our lives!* Now—anyone want to pull out before it's too late?"

There was no answer.

Satan looked at his men long and steadily. "I started out in this chase after what I thought might be profitable, but small, game. Now, however, it's changed. I crossed trails with something else. Something infinitely bigger.

"We're gunning for the United States Government," he said soberly.

There was a stir in the group of men. But no one interrupted.

"I DON'T know exactly where I'm headed yet," Satan went on after a brief pause. "But unless I'm greatly mistaken, we'll all know in very short order. Our quarry suspects us, seems to know that we're in the field. And the Government knows that we're in, too. *Both* the G-men and the gang we're pointing for will be on the watch for us. Is that clear?"

Murmurs of assent came from the crew. Satan nodded and went on:

"There's no question of this being a political matter," he said.

"I have thought it all out, and there's only one conclusion: The Government is being raided by a group, I don't know who, with a view to wrecking it. Already, some of the highest men in Washington have been reached. I know that. But how, or by whom—or what the stake is—I can't guess.

"If it's a gang of master political crooks we'll crush them and take whatever they have. Share and share alike, when we do, on all but my portion. I'll take the usual one-third cut. That agreeable? If it isn't, I want to hear it now!"

Still no voice was raised in the crew. They sat silent, their eyes intent on Captain Satan; eyes that seemed to study, to ponder, to grope....

"You'll get orders to-night. Here. You'll each of you have a job to do before you report back to Slim. As usual, as always, you won't see me unless I call for the meeting. And as always you'll never see me in any other way than I am now." He paused and smiled grimly. "So don't waste your time trying to figure out who I am in any other life—who I might be when I'm not being... Captain Satan!"

Several of the crew flushed guiltily. Slim chuckled.

"One man and one man alone will know me," Satan continued. "That, of course, is Slim. You all remember your emergency call letters? The first and last letter of your Satan's Crew names. For instance, Frenchy's are 'F-Y.' Soapy's, 'S-Y.' Kayo's, 'K-O.' And so on. Don't forget that." He smiled harshly. "Sledge's imitator did!"

He turned toward Slim and stretched out his hand. Slim passed a black leather bag to him, which he opened out onto the floor. He distributed among the crew a number of small, gold badges.

"These are F.B.I. badges," he said. "You'll use them only in cases of extreme emergency, or when Slim otherwise instructs you to. I'm sorry"—he smiled slightly—"I'm sorry that we didn't have time to make each one a different number. You'll notice that they're all one and the same badge. The original belongs to Desher, Chief of the F.B.I."

Soapy grinned. "Some class! The Chief, no less!"

Gentleman Dan yawned. "Be rather embarrassing to use it in a place where Desher was already in conference, wouldn't it? Or to show it to one of Desher's own men? Might lead to trouble."

Satan's eyes glinted with the hard humor of the thing. "Very," he agreed. "But that's up to you men. Use them only in emergency—or under orders!" He pulled a huge wad of bills from the bag. "You'll all have plenty of money to start." His eyes slid to Soapy's bulging ones. "But don't—er—lose it, or use it unnecessarily. Now, all of you listen while you get orders.

"Gentleman Dan! Trace down this dead man. Find where he came from, his name. That's all, mind you! Find out and report back to Slim. Understand?"

"Right, Cap'n."

"Soapy! Get around in the underworld and see if you can get wind of any new 'big shots.'"

"Right, Cap'n."

"Frenchy! I want you to get an interview with King Cal Merrill, the baseball pitcher. Pay him anything you have to, to get it. Tell him you want to write a story about him for foreign newspapers. But what I really want you to do is watch him closely and see if you think he's been fixed up with some drug— or by money!"

"*Oui, monsieur,*" Frenchy grinned. "I'll be the foreign sports correspondent for *Le Figaro.*"

"Right. You, Kayo—you'll drive me, as usual. Mike will work with Slim, stay with him day and night. Happy—I want you to get into the night clubs, the hot spots. You're an out-of-town big spender, and everybody's pal. Keep your eyes and ears open.

"You, Big Bill—cover the docks. Play the drunk, and cover a lot of territory. See if you can get wind of anything that looks new or big. Smuggled shipments out of the country, especially."

"Shipments of what, Cap'n?"

"You wouldn't know," Satan told him. "But it would be guarded closely. I think it'll be"—he paused significantly—"gold!"

"A lot of hush-hush and a heavy guard, huh?" Big Bill nodded.

"Right. Doc, nose around the laboratories and see if you can find a drug—any drug—that will act as a hypnotic agent and defy detection by the closest observers."

"*What?*" The medical man stared, then shook his head slowly. "I can tell you right now to save your time, Cap'n."

"Carry out my orders," Satan snapped. "Now, are we all set? Any questions to be asked?"

Gentleman Dan spoke up. "You said we were gunning for the Government, Cap'n. Did you mean just that? If you do—"

"What's your trouble, Dan? Weren't you listening when I spoke a little while ago? I said that some gang was twisting the government—and I meant just that! I'm going to get that gang; and the mob that I get will pay me for my—er—services. But I'm no traitor!"

His eyes were narrowed when he looked around the group. The seriousness of what he was about to say was obvious to them all.

"I'm very much afraid that a mob has gotten to the government already. And if it has?" He paused significantly. "If it has, then I'll smash the Big Wigs in Washington—if I must—to get at the man behind this thing! That's all, men. Good luck!"

"Happy hunting, Cap'n," Gentleman Dan drawled.

WHEN THE men had filed out, Mike and Kayo, who were staying with the two others, withdrew to a corner, Satan turned to Slim.

"Next week," he said in a low voice. "Here. At the same time."

"Right, Captain." Then, with a tinge of anxiety, "You sure you'll be all right?"

Satan smiled slightly. "I'm going to be very much interested in banking affairs for the next few days, Slim. You see, it's just possible that I might get wind of this gang's money. There's no better way to cripple a big mob than by getting a strangle hold on its bankroll!"

Slim nodded somberly. "Just the same—"

"Just the same," Satan laughed, "I've been looking after myself for these last—How many years has it been, Slim?"

"Plenty," the gaunt man said morosely. "But not without my help," he reminded.

Satan put out his hand and gripped Slim's so hard that the

man winced. "I don't know what I'd do without you, Slim," he said with a catch of emotion in his voice. "Take care of yourself!"

Satan was raising the flap of the improvised tent to leave when Slim's voice stopped him. "Wait, Captain! I *knew* you couldn't look after yourself." He held a sheaf of currency in his hand, a badge on top of it. "You've already lost your badge and your money!"

"You ass," Satan grinned. Slim's mournful face broke into a broad smile.

And Captain Satan was gone.

CHAPTER 5
DANGER TRAIL

S HORTLY AFTER ten o'clock in the morning, a shiny sedan bearing Florida license tags drew up in front of the impressive Atlas Bank & Trust Company's main office. The uniformed doorman sprang to open the rear door of the car.

A blond young man, not impressively dressed, but with pleasant gray eyes that peered out from behind metal spectacles, descended. "Will you show my man where to park?" he inquired. "We're strangers…"

"Leave it to me," the big doorman boomed. "Just you go on inside, sir. I'll show the driver where he can wait."

"Thank you." But the young man hesitated. The doorman looked at him inquiringly. "Er—I'd better wait and see where you put him," he said apologetically. "I'm going to the World Series game today, and I don't want to chance losing my driver."

The doorman laughed. "You've plenty of time for that," he said. But he swung onto the running board and guided the big, burly driver down the street. When he came back, the young man was still waiting.

"You say I've plenty of time?" he asked anxiously.

"Indeed you have. More than three hours. Why, our own boss here, Mr. Mason, didn't leave until after one o'clock yesterday."

"Who? Mr. Mason? Who is he?"

The doorman's eyes were incredulous. "You don't know who Mr. Manse Mason is? The president of the Atlas Bank?"

"Oh," the stranger laughed at himself. "Of course." Then, "Is Mr. Mason a great fan, too?"

The doorman shook his head. "It's news to me if he is," he said. "But he went to the first game, and again yesterday. King Cal lost 'em both, you know." He thought a moment, scratched his chin. "Come to think of it, he probably had a bet down. He was back before the game was over. Seemed upset about something."

The young man nodded and walked slowly up the steps and through the great portals of the place. A special officer saw him looking around and came over. The young man smiled affably.

"Where will I find Mr. Mason? Mr. Manse Mason?"

The Special indicated a man seated at a desk behind an enclosure. "That's his secretary. You'll have to see him first."

Two minutes later, the young stranger was giving his name to the secretary. "I'm Willard Haskell," he said. "Miami, Florida. I'd like to see Mr. Mason."

The secretary fastened a bleak eye on him. "What about?"

"A—er—banking matter."

"Yes, I had presumed that. But, what, exactly, is it?"

"A *personal* banking matter."

A door behind the secretary had opened. A rugged, square-faced man, faultlessly and conservatively dressed in gray, was coming out. The secretary said:

"Unless you tell me your business you can't see Mr. Mason."

"Oh!" The young man from Florida seemed puzzled. "Are you sure of that?"

The big man who had come from the office of the bank paused, his dark eyes taking in the secretary and visitor. But he didn't interrupt.

"Of course I'm sure," the secretary snapped. "Mr. Mason's time isn't to be wasted."

"Oh," a guileless smile broke on the Floridian's face. "He has time for baseball games, but not for the banking business. Is that it?"

The secretary crimsoned. "Just what business of yours—" But a new voice cut in, drowned him out.

"How do you know Mr. Mason has time for baseball games?"

The answer was quiet; but the young man's eyes were full of meaning. "I saw him there yesterday," he said. "Rather—I *thought* I did."

Brown eyes stared long and fixedly into mild gray ones. The browns wavered first. "Come in," the man snapped. "Mr. Mason will see you!"

The stranger who had forced admittance to the offices of one of the greatest bankers in the land smiled his acceptance of the big, dark man's invitation and preceded him.

But his smile froze into bleak hardness a moment later when the door to the private offices clicked shut on the busy desks and cages outside... And something hard was jammed into his back.

"Straight ahead, wise guy," a voice grated in his ear. "I don't know what your game is, but you've pushed it a bit too far!"

Satan shrugged his shoulders and said in a meek voice: "All right, sir."

IT WAS a short, narrow hall that led to a door, perhaps twelve feet down a carpeted way. Satan stopped short of the door and waited for developments.

"Open it," the man with the gun commanded. "And no funny stuff!"

Satan—still very much the mild young man from Florida—did as he was told. He found himself in a large anteroom, beyond which was another door. The heavy, darker man covered Satan with his gun while he pressed a button on the wall near that other door. There was an immediate click.

"Push it open," Satan's captor ordered.

Satan did... and found himself looking into the well known features of Mr. Manse Mason, President of the great Atlas Bank. The portly, florid-faced banker sat quietly at a large, mahogany desk, his hands folded as he watched with puzzled inquiry the two who entered.

"Well, well, Mr. Mesters," he boomed in a jovial voice. "Glad to see you, glad to see you! And this young man—?"

"Cut out the glad hand stuff," Satan's companion snapped. "This yegg was trying to beat his way into your office when I was going out. He's got something up his sleeve. Call your secretary and tell him you aren't to be disturbed." His voice was ominous when he added. "Not before we *dispose* of this business."

Manse Mason frowned, but he picked up his desk 'phone and gave the necessary instructions. When he dropped the receiver back on the hook, the man with the gun shoved Satan into a chair. Then he turned.

"Our young friend here," he said, his voice heavy with irony, "Saw *you* at the ball game yesterday!"

Mason shot a startled look at Satan. He glanced at Mesters. "Er—don't you think, Mesters, that this sort of thing is a bit indiscreet? After all—?"

"Indiscreet?" Mester laughed heavily. "That's a mild word, Mason. After all—" He chuckled and came nearer the desk. "After all, if we're going to worry about being indiscreet, it's time we had a heart to heart discussion about it!"

Mason paled slightly and shifted his gaze. Satan wondered at the implied threat in Mesters' words; but he sat silent, playing his part of the stranger from Florida. Mesters turned.

"*Where* did you see Mason, at the game? In what part of the stands?"

Satan thought quickly. It wouldn't do to give them the impression he knew too much. "In the lower stands," he said easily.

Mason stirred. "You see, Mesters? You're too—you're going off half-cocked on this."

Mesters shook his head. "You didn't even attend the game,"

he said slowly, a smile on his face. "So why would this man say he had seen you unless he knew you had intended to go—but didn't? I tell you, Mason, he *knows* something!"

Mason's good looking face had regained some of its customary floridity. But his eyes were agate-blue when he bent them on Satan again.

"Who are you? What do you want here?"

Satan gave the name again. "Willard Haskell. I'm up from Florida on business. Important business," he added as an after thought. He waited.

Mason and Mesters regarded him silently for a moment. Then:

"What kind of business?" Mesters snapped. "And who says it is important?"

Satan looked at him coolly, then back to Mason. "I find this man exceedingly rude," he said quietly. "Is it the custom of all New York bankers to use gunmen, to threaten callers who come on important investment matters?"

Again Mason shifted uneasily. But Mesters cut in before he could speak. "Don't let him kid you, Mason. He's a phony. If you weren't at the game yesterday, how could he have seen you?" His voice took on meaning when he went on:

"But he knew you had planned to be there!"

Mason stared at Satan for a long moment. "Mesters," he said, "why don't you get Hymie? He thought *you* were being followed yesterday. Remember? Maybe he'd recognize *this* man. If not—" He looked back at Satan. "If not, we've made a dreadful mistake. Don't you see? One that's liable to prove... embarrassing!"

Mesters smiled coldly. "For *him*. Not for us!"

Mason urged him. "Get Hymie!"

Mesters considered a moment, then shrugged. "All right." He put his automatic on the table. "Cover him with this, Mason. And whatever you do, don't let him get away! Understand?"

Mason nodded. Mesters went out and closed the door after him. But a few minutes later, an almost soundless buzz stirred in the little office. Mason reached forward and pressed a button on the desk. The door swung open and Mesters stood there again. But wearing a hat, this time.

Recognition dawned on Satan with stunning force. The man in the doorway was no stranger to him—now! But he dropped his eyes quickly.

"You sure you can handle him?" Mesters asked.

Mason smiled slightly. "Will you get Hymie?"

"I'll call him," Mesters decided suddenly. "Then—"

"Mesters!" Mason's voice was weary. "How often must I remind you that we can't have any connection between this office and Hymie, even by telephone? For God's sake, man—your impatience will ruin everything!"

"Oh, all right." Mesters withdrew, closing the door carefully behind him.

Satan sat with eyes averted, his brain busily recording the things he had seen and heard…

…Mason, the great banker, taking orders from a gunman!… Mason was supposed to be at the ball game… But, he hadn't been. Satan had gathered that much from the conversation of the two men.

50

…Satan remembered that Soapy had traced two men from that ball park to this bank. Obviously, Mason hadn't been one of those men, or Soapy would have said so. Mason was too well known a figure to go unrecognized. Yet, the doorman outside had said: " 'Mr. Mason was a bit upset when he came back.' "

Satan filed the facts away for future thought. But he looked up with a slight smile at this thought. *Would* there be any future?

The banker was watching him. "What's so funny?" the big man growled.

"I was just thinking," Satan said evenly. "I was just thinking that *your* game—whatever it is—must be pretty risky, pretty big, to have you so jumpy that you employ gunmen to meet your casual callers!"

Mason blinked and looked away. Satan followed up, "Do you mind if I show you something? Something I have in my pocket?" At the look that crossed Mason's face: "I'm not armed."

Mason said, "Go ahead. But try anything and—" He wagged the gun menacingly. Gingerly, Satan reached into his pocket and fished out his fake F.B.I. badge. But before passing it to Mason, he fetched a gold cigarette case and selected a cigarette.

"Have one?"

Mason shook his head, his guard still alert. "What is it you want to show me?"

"You see," Satan said, drawing a flat pocket-lighter from his vest, "I didn't want to show you this in front of—Mesters. That his name?"

Mason nodded. "What have you to show me?"

Satan tossed the F.B.I. badge to the desk. Mason's face broke

51

into a broad smile when he saw what it was. "Now, Haskell—or whatever you call yourself—don't you know that this is going to get you in trouble? All I've got to do is to call—"

He looked up suddenly. Satan had dropped one hand—the hand that held the cigarette lighter—to his side and reversed the lighter, pointing the bottom of it past Mason's desk. He pressed a small button on the side… and let his eyes widen in simulated horror as they fastened on the image that sprang into being on the dark panelled wall.

Mason swung slightly, then froze in his chair, his eyes starting and his mouth dropping wide. In a spot of light on the wall stood the satanic head and upraised pitchfork that was Satan's trademark.

Mason gasped. "Captain Satan! My God, where—"

At that same instant, Satan struck.

SATAN RUBBED his knuckles and stared at the banker. Mason was slumped in his chair, a knockout blow to the point of the chin having done the trick. For a moment, Satan listened for any sounds from outside. Then he crossed swiftly to the banker's small, private safe, standing in a corner of the spacious room.

He dropped to his knees and twirled the dial tentatively, now right, now left. His head was bent and the fingers of his left hand were resting lightly on the dial housing to detect any fall of the tumblers that he couldn't hear.

In another minute he swung the door of the thing open.

He didn't disturb the small pile of banknotes there; nor the promisory notes, indorsed to the banker personally, other than to glance through them hurriedly.

"Loans to friends," Satan guessed after reading a cryptic but amusing notation regarding a defaulted payment.

"*A Mavourneen loan.*" was written in pencil. "*It may be a day, and it may be forever!*"

A small cubby-drawer was locked. Satan slipped a slender jimmy from his inside pocket and pried it open. His face lighted when he saw the letterheads. "The Secretary of the Treasury!" he breathed.

Quickly, he stuffed the letters in his pocket, then closed the safe again. He walked over and took up a position back of the unconscious banker's chair. After a moment's reflection, he put both hands to his own hair and tugged gently but firmly. The wig came off his closely shaved head.

Working rapidly, he picked the table shears from the big mahogany desk and grabbed the banker's generous thatch of graying hair with a rough hand. Twenty snips of the sharp bladed cutters and Mason looked like a plucked turkey. With a grin, Satan adjusted the blond wig and looked at the man critically.

Mason stirred suddenly. Satan bent lover and picked up the gun. One well aimed *thwack* and the banker went back to sleep. Satan plucked the spectacles from his own nose and adjusted them on the banker.

As a last thought, he plucked a pen from its holder on the desk and sketched hurriedly the Satan-and-pitchfork device on the man's forehead.

"I don't know where you fit into this picture, old boy," he murmured as he snapped his hat on, "but it's a cinch you're mixed in something pretty deep. And it's an easier guess that your pal Mesters is in even deeper! Maybe this'll set you to jittering and drive you into the open!"

He frowned at the recollection of Mason's laugh when the banker had seen the F.B.I. badge. "...Don't you know this is going to get you into trouble...?" the man's words had been.

"They must be in strong with the Department of Justice," Satan guessed. "Or with someone even higher!"

He realized with a sudden shock that he might be barking up the wrong orchard; or, that even if he weren't—even if he *had* stumbled on something—that the odds against him were tremendous. The whole resources of the Government—granted even that it was a crooked Government, or at the moment in the hands of some unscrupulous ring—would be pitted against him. *Plus* the canny, invisible powers who were pulling the strings.

"I'll have to move," he muttered. "I can't afford to get caught in here."

His eyes went to the window, the heavily curtained window, at the end of the room. But he knew even before he pulled back the hangings that it would be barred. There was no exit there.

"Oh, well. It'll be simple enough for me to just walk out the way I came in."

And just then the buzzer sounded in the office... the buzzer that told Satan that the man Mesters was back—with Hymie!

CHAPTER 6
SATAN'S SANCTUARY

S ATAN STOOD rooted near the window. But his mind raced ahead with a plan. The door opened in such a manner that the men who entered would see the banker before they could see *him*, if he stood behind the door. But he couldn't do that and still hold the buzzer to let them in. And if he didn't hold the buzzer, didn't answer the signal—

"They'll call guards to break it in, and then I'm fixed for sure!"

He jumped to the desk and found a heavy book there. He set this on the buzzer button and slithered back beyond the door. It swung open almost instantly.

Mesters had been talking as he entered. Satan recognized the voice even as the door swung open. But the man broke off in his speech at the sight of the blond, bespectacled figure in the banker's chair.

"What the—?"

Mesters hurried in, and a small, furtive-faced man followed him. Satan moved fast. His gun hand rose and fell and the furtive one slid to the floor without so much as a groan.

But Mesters had whipped around at the sound of the gun hitting the man's head. The big man's hand jumped for his hip pocket, but Satan jumped faster. His left hand whipped up in a short arc and staggered Mesters back two feet.

Stepping swiftly, Satan followed up his advantage. He dug a fist into the big man's midriff, then crossed the butt of the gun hard to the jaw. Mesters went down.

Satan started away. Then he stopped, came back swiftly to Mesters and ripped the man's jacket open. He appropriated the wallet and papers he saw there and stood again. The little man who had come in with Mesters—Hymie—was coming to. Satan stepped over him and into the anteroom, pulling the door shut after him.

Down the corridor to the door leading into the main part of the bank he raced. But when he pushed the door open he was walking very sedately. He ignored the inquiring glance of the secretary and made his way through the other desks and into the main aisle.

But he was only halfway to the street when he heard that door behind him burst open.

"Stop that man!" he heard the hoarse cry. "Stop—that—man!"

A special officer looked at Satan, then sprang for him. Satan gripped him with a steely hand. "Not me, you fool! *That* man!" He pointed to a small man who was just leaving the building.

He yanked the Special and ran, the sound of bedlam rising behind him. When his body was screened from the street by a huge pillar, he stopped and swung on the Special. The man dropped and Satan broke for the portals.

A shot sounded from inside as he skittered down the steps. The genial doorman, who had been so informative before, turned at the sound of the shot. He made a grab for Satan.

"It's a hold up!" Satan snapped. "Get in there with your gun and help then. I'll call the police."

The ruse worked. The doorman bounded up the steps with astonishing agility for a heavy man. But before he was halfway up, Satan was streaking down B r o a d w a y toward his sedan at top speed. As he went, he whistled three shrill blasts through his lips.

The sedan's motor was thrumming with impatient power when Satan swarmed through the door Kayo had obligingly left open.

"Step on it! Down the one-way street, next corner—the *wrong* way!" He looked back through the rear window. "Did you change the license plates?"

"Sure thing, Cap'n," Kayo said as he slid into second and took the corner on two wheels. "We're from Ohio, for now."

Kayo piloted the car at a dizzy pace down the one-way street and skidded expertly right and left to avoid, by a hair, the cars coming the other way—the right way. Drivers cursed and slammed on their brakes. Pedestrians swore and shook their fists.

But Kayo bolted ahead. A police siren was sounding when they came to the next intersection.

"Turn right and double back," Satan snapped.

"Right, Cap'n."

The car careened around the corner, narrowly missing a truck, and leapt ahead for the next corner like a frightened antelope. The tires screamed in agony when Kayo bent the wheel hard. At Broadway, they turned right again.

A huge throng was jammed in front of the Atlas Bank. Police cars were rolling up, their sirens moaning and their doors disgorging police. Satan's eyes went hard when he made out the figure of the big doorman standing in a circle of police.

"Park right here!" he snapped.

"Cheez—er—I mean, yes, Cap'n," Kayo corrected himself hastily. His face was pasty when he pulled in to the curb directly across the street from the bank.

"You needn't wait," Satan said casually when he had descended and slammed the door. "I'll see you at the—at *home*. Put the car up and wait there for me."

"Yes, Cap'n."

The big sedan slid away. Satan walked up the steps of a building directly across the street from the bank, pushing his way gently but surely through the crowd on the steps.

"What's wrong?" he asked a sharp eyed man who was scanning the nearby crowds.

"G'wan about your business," the man said from the side of his mouth.

Satan laughed. "What's wrong with my asking that? You don't need to get so—"

"Scram!" the man snapped, his eyes boring into Satan. He flashed a hand from his pocket, opened it to show a badge.

"Excuse me," murmured Satan.

A lad standing nearby grinned. "It's a holdup, or something," he said. "There was shootin' and everything!"

Satan walked inside the lobby and scanned the place. Then he retraced his steps, having found there was a rear exit to the building. He went out to the street and stood next to the police plainclothes-man.

SATAN EDGED back slightly when he saw a new figure emerge from the crowd at the bank door. It was Mesters. The big man went into conference with some of the policemen. Then two automobiles drove up. Mesters went over and talked to the men in the car. Satan noted the license tags. One was a New York car, the other a District of Columbia vehicle.

He wrote down the numbers, watched while two news cameramen came close and snapped pictures of the bank door, the crowds, then of Mesters. One of the photographers craned his neck and looked around. Then he crossed the street and came directly to the steps where Satan was standing. He secured a vantage point where he could get a clear shot of the crowd across the street.

Satan watched the man closely. He wondered what those shots would show—the pictures the man had taken of Mesters and his friends. The cameraman, his work apparently completed, turned. Satan caught his eye and signaled him over and into the lobby.

"You want to get a couple of swell shots?" he asked, leaning close.

"Do I? Why the hell not?" the man said, staring.

"Then," Satan said in a low, even voice, "just let one peep out of you! You'll get some of the best shots you've ever been up against!" He made a significant move with the hand that was buried in his coat pocket. "Walk down here to the back entrance."

"What's the game?" the man protested feebly. But he moved obediently when Satan's hand pushed the coat pocket straight out at him.

The two walked through the oblivious crowd and made their way through the lobby of the big building, down the stairs that led to Church Street, then along Church Street to the next corner. There was a subway entrance there.

Satan stopped. A train was roaring into the station. "See if you can run down these steps faster than I can shoot," he snapped. He took the man's camera.

The cameraman flashed a frightened look and started down the steps. But he had seen through Satan's plan. As he went, he snapped a quick look over his shoulder.

Satan was in full flight down the street, the camera swinging from his left hand. The photo hawk came back to the street level.

"Robber! Police! Stop that guy," he shouted, trailing at a safe distance.

One or two men made a grab at Satan, but he beat them off. He dashed down the side street with the noise of the new chase growing behind him.

"I can't get caught *here*," he knew. "The police at the bank would get a look at me!" He redoubled his efforts, but a shot behind him sent a slug whistling past his ear. Satan looked over his shoulder. A policeman had joined the chase. No; *two* of them!

Another shot came closer, then Satan saw an alley opening to his right. He dodged into it. But he hadn't gone twenty steps before he realized he was trapped. It was a dead end!

He stopped, the sounds of the pursuit loud and close.

And in that moment a voice sounded so close to his ear that he nearly dropped the camera. It was a feminine voice, young, clear, half amused.

"Would you care to step in here for a moment?"

Satan stared. The quick glance he caught was of a girl in the doorway of an old fashioned, two story house. A girl with auburn hair, soft brown eyes, and a sweetly sad, oval face.

He didn't have time for any more. With a gasp of relief, he swarmed up the two steps and past the girl. There was a room on the right, a room with shades drawn, dark. Satan jumped in—and slammed full force into something.

He recoiled from the shock, realizing as he did so that it was a piano he had struck against. Or a moving case. He peered in the dim light of the place and saw that his last surmise was right. It was a huge packing case.

Satan stepped behind it and crouched to the floor. A moment later the pursuers pounded around the corner. He listened, hoping to hear them pound by, hoping against certain knowledge that the girl had stepped back from the door, shut it.

A harsh voice called, "You see a man run down this way, lady?"

Satan's heart fell when he heard the answer, clear and sure.

"Yes. I saw him. Do you want to know where he is?"

HE HALF rose from his crouch, planning to make a dash for the back of the house when the girl would lead the police in. But he exhaled with relief a second later. The girl was speaking.

"That house across the street.... See the little black door? Well, that's an alley which runs through to the next north and south street. But he's probably—"

"Come on," a gruff voice broke in on her. Feet pounded anew as the chase swept away and out of hearing.

The girl came in and shut the door. She snapped the light switch in the room where Satan was concealed. The fugitive came from behind the packing case and doffed his hat, his eyes taking in the disorder of the room.

Besides the packing case that had nearly floored Satan, there were a number of smaller ones, all apparently packed in great haste. His eyes swept over them, then came back to the girl. Her eyes were on his head; accusingly.

Satan stared, then grinned when he realized. "Don't let my shaved head worry you, Miss," he said quietly. "I'm not an escaped convict."

The girl smiled slightly. Her eyes had seen the camera. "You're a newsman? You've been taking pictures that the police forbade. Is that it?"

Satan started to answer her in the affirmative. But he found himself reluctant to do so. "No; I'm not," he said simply.

"Oh." The girl's eyes were suddenly troubled. "But—that's your camera?"

Satan shook his head. "I'm afraid it isn't. I—there were some pictures that I wanted. I—er—borrowed the camera from a news photographer." He added hurriedly, "Of course, I am going to return it after I develop the prints."

The girl frowned. "Why not wait until the paper is published, if that's all it is?"

Satan explained. "In all probability, the pictures I want would never appear. Not half the shots taken are used, anyway. And I have reason to believe that these I am interested in might even be suppressed."

"Oh." She thought a moment. "Will—will your developing those pictures hurt anyone?"

Satan was never more serious or convincing in his life. "On the contrary, I can assure you that these pictures may very well benefit—" He paused, decided to hold back what he had started to say: "It will help the United States." It sounded too much like flag waving, like a false appeal to patriotism.

"These pictures will be a great benefit to me," he finished, with a disarming grin.

The girl smiled suddenly. "I believe you. I had a feeling when I saw you running and heard them chasing you, that you were—well, that you weren't a thief. My name is Marianne Sarno," she added.

Satan stirred and looked away. "Miss Sarno, I'm sorry I can't tell you who I am. My name, I mean. I can't tell you my name or reveal my identity without violating a—er—trust. And I don't want to lie to you."

"I like that," the girl said impulsively. "There's so much lying and deceit going on—" She stopped, a strange expression on her face. Then she brightened and said, "I'd rather have it the way it is than to have you lie to me."

Satan put out his hand on an impulse. Marianne Sarno's hand was cool and firm in his when she accepted it. "You've done me a great service," he said seriously. "A very great service, Miss Sarno. I hope some day that I can repay it."

The girl smiled and waved her hand around at the packing cases. "As you see, we're moving. My father and I." Satan thought that her brow clouded for a moment. But she went on quickly. "Dad is a great dermatologist, and has been offered a marvelous opportunity in Washington."

"A dermatologist? That's a skin specialist, isn't it?"

"Yes. He's a skin and hair specialist. Professor Sarno, most of his friends call him. But he's really a doctor. Of late years he's been lecturing on skin disorders and treatment. But now he has a fine chance to do special research work in Washington." The girl paused and stared out into the hall a moment. When she turned again her face was slightly pale and her eyes frightened.

"But I'm afraid," she whispered through tight lips.

Satan blinked. "Afraid? Afraid of what?"

Marianne Sarno shook her head slightly and forced a laugh. But she was visibly shaken. "Oh, you wouldn't understand," she said. "It's probably only my imagination. Nerves, maybe; from being cooped up here in dad's laboratory all the time. You see, I help with his research work."

"Oh." But Satan was puzzled.

"It's not that the work is dangerous in itself. It's—" she paused, as if fighting with her sense of loyalty to her father. "It's dad's new friends—the people who are backing him in this thing. I… don't like them."

Satan considered. "Who are they? Why don't you like them?"

"I'm going to plead as you did a minute ago," Marianne Sarno smiled wanly. "I can't tell you who they are, without violating a trust. A sacred trust. I promised dad, you see."

Satan shrugged. "Let's hope your womanly intuition has called the shot wrong," he smiled. The noises in the street outside had subsided. Soon the noon lunch crowds would be pouring out of the skyscrapers and Satan could easily lose himself in them and get away to safer environs. "Where are you moving to?"

"I can't tell you that, either," Marianne said. There was a sudden sound at the door and the girl gasped. Satan found himself looking into the face of one of the strangest men he had ever seen.

Short and weazened, he was—sparrowlike, almost, in his stature. Great but lifeless brown eyes stared out of a thin, ascetic, kind face. His hair was long and wispy-gray and brushed straight back from his high, intelligent forehead.

"Who is this young man, Marianne?" he asked in a reedy, detached voice. It was as if he were walking in his sleep, so indifferent were his eyes, so far away his voice.

"He's—a young man who came to take some things we didn't need, father."

"Ah, yes." 'Professor' Sarno stared at Satan again. "You

shouldn't shave your head, young man." He came closer. "Not with such *good* hair, especially. Ah, yes! I can see, even though you have so little hair, that it is *good* hair." His eyes ranged down to Satan's face.

"You are an outdoor man, I can see. An adventurer, perhaps, of some sort? I can see that in your eyes. But do not stay too much in the sun. It is bad, staying too much in the sun and the winds." He turned to Marianne, who had stood there silently.

"You have told him nothing?"

Captain Satan

"I have told him nothing, father."

"That is good, Marianne. It would not do to tell. Remember our great trust, Marianne!" And the man was gone as soundlessly as he had come.

Satan knew, somehow, that this situation was even more strange than it had first appeared. He was on the point of asking again where Marianne and her father, Professor Sarno, were moving to. He had a queer hunch—but he gave it up with a shrug.

He was stooping to pick up the purloined camera, when his eye caught an address tag on the packing case—a tag that was neatly printed in a feminine hand.

Marianne Sarno, it read. The name was followed by an address on *N Street, Washington, D.C.*

He smiled slightly when he saw it, etched it into his memory. When he straightened he found Marianne's eyes on him. He thought that they were suddenly bright, glad.

"I didn't tell you anything," she said, blushing.

"Not a thing in the world," Satan assured her heartily. But he was grinning broadly when he put out his hand.

"Thank you, Marianne. I can't tell you how much you've helped me." His eyes glittered when he added: "Who knows but that your help may be the means of my making perhaps a million dollars!"

He slipped down the alley and into the street unobserved. Five minutes later, he was talking from an out-of-the-way 'phone booth.

"Special meeting for to-morrow night," he said. "Have everyone there. I'm slipping off to get a good long sleep and go over some papers and photos I came across."

"The Atlas Bank was stuck up by a crazy man, Captain," Slim's voice said evenly. "But he didn't take anything."

Satan chuckled. "That's what the bank says!"

"He didn't take anything, Captain," Slim's voice continued. "But he *left* something!"

Satan's face tightened. "Good God! What was left there?"

"An F.B.I. badge. Soapy got the dope from a stoolie he knows!"

BACK AT the Atlas Bank, Mesters, slightly the worse for wear, was closeted in secret conference with the bedraggled looking Manse Mason.

"That's the whole situation, Mason," Mesters was saying as he paced the floor. "Desher is on his way up from Washington now. He lost his badge, or had it stolen, while he was here in New York. He had no more to do with this man who was here—this *Satan*," he fairly spat out the sobriquet—"than I had."

Mason passed a restless hand over his once ample thatch, He snatched it away again. "I want him broken, anyway. Imagine a G-man losing his badge. And losing it to Satan, of all people!"

Mesters considered. "Well, we got it back. I'd rather know that Desher had it than that Satan was still floating around with it, using it."

"I want Desher broken," Mason persisted.

The big man ceased his pacing. His eyes were ugly when they rested on Mason. "I've had about enough of this talk of what *you* want," he said through set teeth. "Desher stays untouched.

Why, you damn fool, I can't even stay and meet the man! *You* know that! So how in hell do you think I'm going to break him?" You must be crazy, Mason!"

Mason shook his head despairingly. "But—my hair? Look at it! Do you still think I can get away with—?" He paused at the look of warning that Mesters flashed him.

Mesters said, at last. "Keep your shirt on and play your part. Remember *I'm* boss here!"

Mason sat in miserable silence. But he looked up at the hearty chuckle that came from his companion. "Well? For God's sake, if you know anything funny tell it to me!"

"Look in the mirror," Mesters choked. "Manse Mason, eh?"

"Go to hell," Mason growled.

CHAPTER 7
THE DEVIL THROWS THE DICE

S ATAN WAS adamant that the meeting be held at the old rendezvous. Slim pointed out that since the false Sledge had found the meeting place, so might others.

"We'll be at the same place," Satan insisted. "We'll post guards in advance and during the meeting. This mob isn't going to drive me out of my base of operations."

"Right, Captain," Slim gave in.

The meeting opened with its customary speed and privacy, however. In the contrived shelter within the deserted warehouse, Satan took his place on an upended box and called for reports.

Gentleman Dan spoke first. "Traced your man, Cap'n," he

drawled. "My tailor gave me a lead on where I could check the cloth of his suit. It was imported stuff. At least, not of American make. I telephoned the manufacturers after I had made an analysis of the material. It chanced that it was a batch of goods made expressly for Canadian tailors, by an English house." He paused, then continued:

"So, the man obviously'd had the suit made in Canada. I had snapped a picture of Sledge once, I remembered. I got it out of an album and took a plane to Montreal: no soap. I flew to Quebec: no soap. I flew to Toronto: success. Your man is— *was*—one Dokey Martin, ex-pug, ex-confidence man, ex-Capone gangster." He frowned.

"Well?" Satan prompted him.

"Here's the odd part of it," Gentleman Dan said slowly. "Martin was a blue-eyed blond. Sledge was a dark-eyed man with black hair. Yet, this man was Sledge."

There was a murmur of surprise from the crew. Satan silenced them. "Martin, in the old days, could have been blond—could have dyed his hair? He might be remembered as blue-eyed when, in reality, he wasn't? Memory plays strange tricks, Dan."

Gentleman Dan shook his good looking head. "He had a police record, Cap'n. I checked it. Blue eyes. Blond hair. Even when he came out of jail he had blond hair, and they don't use hair dye in the big houses. Not any that *I've* been in."

Satan considered. "Then this man wasn't Martin."

Gentleman Dan yawned. "I took finger prints from the stiff before I went. They check—perfectly—with Martin's."

Satan frowned. "He's Martin—but he isn't Martin." He

thought for a moment. "It's not a nice job, but I'd like to have the hair of the—"

Gentleman Dan interrupted. "Hair and eyes of the Martin stiff were checked on my return, Cap'n," he said. "Dark eyes, black hair; guaranteed wash proof."

Satan nodded. "Good work. Dan." He turned to Slim. "Gentleman Dan gets a five hundred bonus, out of my share, Slim. Mark it down. Who's next?" he asked.

Big Bill spoke up. "Of course, I haven't been working long, Cap'n. But there's not a peep going around about any smuggling shipments. Not a peep. And where I've been, they'd know!"

Soapy put in his bit. "I got the office that a new mob is snapping up trigger men, Cap'n. It's off the record what mob it is. But I'll know soon. And another thing, too—"

"What?"

"It's being whispered around that some big bank is going to be loaded for a record touch, some day soon. But the thing is very much on the hush-hush." Soapy smiled slightly. "I'm to get a bit of it when it cracks."

"What bank is it, Soapy?"

"Dunno, Cap'n," Soapy said regretfully. "All I know is that a guy named Hymie, a trigger man from out west, is doin' the set-up for it."

"*Hymie!* Did you see him?"

"Not yet, Cap'n. I talked with a lad who is doin' the hirin'— under him. It's to be a big, super-special crack job, with all the trimmin's."

Satan thought for a minute. "Soapy—did you lose sight of

that car you followed from the game the other day? To the Atlas Bank? Think hard now, Soapy!"

The little man flushed. "To tell the truth, Can'n—we come to a bad traffic jam an' I'm lookin' out the window an' see a swell jane. You know; a girl. I'm lookin' her over a bit, when I hear something slam. I turn and think I see a guy walking away from the car I'm tailin'. And I *think* a new gent had got in it."

Satan nodded slowly, a hard smile stretching his lips. "I thought so! Was the man walking away from that car small and dark? Slinky, sort of? And the man you hadn't seen before—the new man—big, and red-faced, and well dressed?"

Soapy nodded miserably. Satan turned to Slim. "Fine Soapy another thousand dollars, Slim. Next?"

Frenchy spoke up. "I tried to interview King Cal, and got everything but the home plate fired at me. Then some strong arm guys muscled me out of there. But I got a good look at King Cal."

"Notice anything strange?"

"Not especially. He just struck me as being sore as hell."

Satan's face was tense with excitement, King Cal was self-control personified.

"I think we're getting somewhere, at—"

Two shots rang out from nearby. "Mike's in trouble," Kayo called in to Satan. "Two guys were snooping around, so he followed them."

The crew broke from cover of the shelter, automatics jumping as if by magic into a half-dozen hands. As he ran, Satan snapped, "Why in hell didn't you go, too?"

72

Kayo panted, "Cap'n, my orders were to stand guard at this door, inside. And not to leave it! I—*Look out!*"

There was a spurt of orange flame in the inky blackness of the pier entrance, and a machine gun

chattered horribly. Satan blasted his automatic into the heart of the fire, saw it waver, smashed it out of being with another volley.

The crew raced on over two shadows that melted into the floor. Slim was in the lead. He stopped suddenly, his eyes on a heap of clothing in the gutter.

"Mike," he said simply. "They got him, Cap'n."

"Pick him up," Satan snapped. "Get those others, too. The cops will be here any minute. Start the engine in the boat and load 'em all aboard."

Three minutes later, a long, all-but-silent power boat stole from under cover of the wharf and sped into the dark reaches of the river. Its lights were shrouded against detection and it seemed no more than a shadow, so low did it ride on the water.

Its wake was still alive on the dark water when the first police siren screamed along West Street and moaned to a stop near the deserted wharf.

THE BOAT sped through the night, out into the bay. Three still bodies lay in the rear cockpit. In the fore cabin, lights carefully wrapped to give a minimum of light to outside observers, sat a grim Satan's crew.

"Our meeting place will be changed," Satan said through tight lips. "Slim warned me this might happen, but I had to know. I had to know if the man who tried to pose as Sledge was a lone wolf—or if he had a mob behind him."

Frenchy spoke up. "Where'll we meet after this, Cap'n?"

Satan didn't look at him. "Slim will cover that. Another thing—you men won't contact him any more. He'll contact you. He'll know where a message can reach you."

Slim raised puzzled eyebrows and his glance traveled over the men. But his face was otherwise morosely inexpressive.

"Orders are the same as before," Satan went on. "Keep your eyes and ears open. Any questions?"

There weren't. Satan stood and walked to the companionway. He turned. "Slim—Soapy." The two men followed him up the steps and aft. At a sign, Slim stepped into the rear pit and bent over. He lifted a form in his arms, tenderly, passed it out to Soapy and Satan. Mike was lowered to the deck gently.

Then Slim hurled the corpses of the other two men up from the cockpit to the deck. He climbed out.

Satan turned the rays of his pocket flash on the three dead men. The face of the man Mike was composed in death, smiling slightly. Satan bent and closed the lids over those dead eyes.

His mind went back to the many times he and Mike had worked together.

"Poor Mike," he said in a low voice. "There's one man who never could be a rat." His eyes met Slim's for a long moment. His lieutenant stepped closer.

"You think—?" He paused as if unwilling to say it; but he had to. "You think that one of the crew is against us?"

"I know it," Satan said simply. "They knew of the meeting, this other crowd. They knew enough to decoy a guard away from the door, then to rush us. Rush us in the dark, mind you! So they must have the layout down pretty well, Slim."

Slim nodded. "It's good we posted two guards," he said. "If Kayo hadn't stood his post, those gunners would have been in on us as soon as Mike went down the street."

Soapy, who had been standing near Mike, looked over as the rays of Satan's flash fell again on the dead gunmen. He gasped.

"It's—it's Mugsy the Fish!"

"Quiet!" Satan snapped. Then: "You know one of those men?"

"I sure do, Cap'n," Soapy averred. "He's the guy promised me the job on that bank!"

Satan's and Slim's eyes slid together again, momentarily. Slim came closer. "Let's pressure the bunch that's left," he whispered. "This is getting too risky, Captain."

Satan shook his head. "Then the spy in our crowd would know that we were on to him. He'd break for cover. I've *got* to know whose mob this is we're up against, Slim. I'll have to track the rat down in some way so that he won't suspect we're on to him. And when I do—" He paused and smiled darkly. "When

I do find him, I think I know how to handle him." He turned to Soapy.

"Think you can get on the track of this bank job again? Can you contact the bunch that this Mugsy the Fish runs with and get to Hymie?"

Soapy shook his head. "I don't know how. Mugsy was a cagey worker. I don't know any of his pals. And Hymie is a mysterious gent, even to Mugsy."

"That fixes *that*," Satan murmured. "Know the other man?"

Soapy bent and stared, focusing the ray of the spotlight. "Never saw him in my life."

Satan nodded. "Get another lead on Hymie, now that this man—The Fish, you called him—is gone."

Soapy shrugged. "I'll go to work again, Cap'n."

Satan said to Slim, "Get the flag from the chest in the cabin, will you? I think Mike would like it that way. And call the boys out here right away."

Under the dark of a starless night, Satan and Slim tenderly wrapped Mike's form in the American flag. They weighted the shroud down with the spare anchor, tying it securely about Mike's shoulders and legs.

Satan stood with bent head for a moment. When he looked up his eyes were far away.

He faced the shrouded figure and came to a sober salute.

"Happy hunting, Mike."

"Amen," Satan's crew chorused solemnly.

"Lower away, men," Satan said in a subdued voice. Slim and Kayo, Mike's two cronies in the crew, performed this last office for their friend. The waters of New York Bay closed noiselessly over Satan's dead.

Satan turned to the others with a snarl. "Throw those two rats overboard!"

THE BOAT was nosed back for port again. Satan and Slim stood alone on the fore deck, the breeze of the early morning blowing a freshening gale in their faces.

"Slim," Satan said after a long silence. "I'm going to shoot the works. I'm going to gamble everything on a hunch I have."

"What's that, Captain?"

"I'm going to do a bit of investigating on my own again. But I'm very much afraid that we'll have to move fast—to shoot first and ask questions later. This opposition gang is getting desperate."

Slim nodded. He had listened to Satan's account of his adventures at the bank, and of Marianne Sarno's aid. "For reasons we both know," Satan told him, "I'm telling only you of this. The others aren't to hear it."

Slim nodded expectantly.

Satan said, "Get ready for a surprise, Slim. All hell's going to pop loose before another twenty-four hours!"

CHAPTER 8
SATAN'S HOSTAGE

A T A sign from Satan, the black limousine slid to a stop on a darkened upper-East Side street. "Don't move, Kayo. Stay right here. Disregard any shots that may be fired. Under no circumstances leave unless I fire three times, then shout your emergency letters. Understand?"

"Yes, Cap'n."

In his silk hat, white muffler, black coat and evening clothes, Satan might have been one of a hundred other social bloods out on a pleasure round.

Excepting that Satan disdained the rich front entrance of the private house near which Kayo had parked. Instead, he fitted a skeleton key to an iron-grilled service door and disappeared into that.

At the end of a short alley, and treading lightly but surely, Satan came to a high fence with spiked top. He stooped low and raised an improvised ladder from where it lay in the dark of the alley; a ladder that was remarkably like the scaling ladders used by fire departments.

He fitted the hooked ends to the fence and went up the thing with the agility of a monkey. At the top, he fitted his feet carefully between two of the sharp spikes and raised the ladder. He dropped it down the other side and clambered down into the rear yard.

It was well after the dinner hour, and Satan knew that the servants in the big house would be through their kitchen chores. They'd be either in their bedrooms or out of the house. The houseman might still be on duty.

Calmly, unhurriedly, Satan fitted keys to the darkened kitchen door until he found one that did the job. He pushed the door open, stopped patiently to open another. He closed them noiselessly after him… but didn't lock them.

His flashlight showed him the way through the kitchen tables in the big room. He went forward slowly but confidently, with all the assuredness of an invited guest. He found the door leading upstairs. That, too, was locked.

Satan managed it as he had managed the others. Voices came to him from a room somewhere above as he ascended quietly, unhurriedly. The first floor of the house was in darkness, save for a light burning in the foyer entrance. Satan looked about him with alert eyes before he started for the second floor.

The voices were clear, now. A young girl was speaking....

"...But, Mama—you promised me, you know! You and Daddy were going to Florida with me *early*."

An older voice—infinitely older, tired, distraught—spoke. "But I'm trying to tell you, Suzy, that your father has changed his mind!"

"If you ask me," the 'Suzy' voice put in petulantly, "Daddy's changed so utterly that he's no fun at all, any more! I think it's perfectly—"

Satan smiled thinly. But he paused not an instant in his climbing of the stairs. 'Suzy' was still in the midst of her complaints of maltreatment from her father, when Satan walked soundlessly into the richly furnished room that was Banker Mason's pride and boast.

Two feminine gasps greeted his unheralded appearance. Satan removed his topper for the first time, bowed low to an elderly woman who was now sitting bolt upright in a gold and brocade chair.

He turned and bowed to a pert-nosed sub-deb who was stretched languidly on a sofa.

"Good evening," he smiled brightly, clicking his heels and snapping his shaved head smartly. "I seem to have arrived at a most timely moment. You are discussing, I believe, the husband of one and the father of the other of you two charming ladies— Mr. Manse Mason?"

Mrs. Mason struggled to rise. "Why, this is preposterous! Who are you sir? Do you know him, Suzy? No, of course you don't! How did you gain entrance, may I ask?" She opened her ample mouth wide, as if to call for help.

"Don't do that." Satan said softly but ominously. Mrs. Mason stared a stunned moment, fright coming into her eyes. Then she dissolved into silent tears.

"I do believe I'm going completely insane," she sniffed. "This— after all my other troubles!"

Suzy Mason giggled. "He's military, mother! Positively! See—the head?"

Mrs. Mason glared. "A convict, *I* should judge."

Satan smiled. "May I sit down and talk?"

"I don't see how we can very well stop you! Forcing yourself in like this. Who *are* you?"

Satan's face sobered. He fixed Mrs. Mason with a steady eye, then turned his attention to Suzy for a like time. When he spoke it was quietly, gravely.

"I have come to talk to you about—" he paused a long moment—"About your husband's strange actions of late, Mrs. Mason!"

Mrs. Mason tried to glare. But Suzy punctured her last defenses.

"That's sense, Mama," the girl said with the brutal incisiveness of youth. "We've both been talking about hardly anything else for the past few days. *Talk* to the man!"

MRS. MASON was obviously struggling for composure. But her eyes were not trusting when they regarded Satan. Rather, they were suspicious and accusing.

"What is it you want to know?"

"First," Satan said, dropping into a chair and crossing his legs easily, "when did you first notice that he had been acting strangely? Then, has he been sick? Have you changed cooks? And, finally, *how* has he changed?"

"I don't know why I should discuss my husband with a total stranger," Mrs. Mason murmured, with a last attempt to retain some shreds of dignity.

Suzy cut in. "He's been acting positively haywire since—" She calculated with narrowed eyes. "Since four days ago."

"Three," her mother corrected.

"Four," Suzy insisted. "You've got three days on your mind because that's when he moved into his own set of rooms. You don't see him so very often, now."

"Suzy!" Mrs. Mason snapped. "Not another word from you!" She turned to Satan. "At any rate, it was the time he went to that baseball game."

Satan's eyebrows went up. "Then he *did* go to the game? And he has been acting peculiarly ever since?"

"Ever since?" Mrs. Mason echoed. "Why, he acted strangely

in going to the game at all! He never spoke of baseball before, and he's spoken of little else since."

Satan was puzzled. "In what way does he speak of baseball?"

Mrs. Mason threw up her hands in despair. "Suzy, who is that dreadful Prince Somebody-or-other he is always babbling about?"

"King Cal," Suzy corrected. "He's searching the papers for news of his pitching, reading what everyone has to say of him; even mumbling to himself about him at dinner."

Satan whistled softly. There was a glitter in his eyes. "Interesting," he murmured. Then: "Your husband is at a small dinner at the Vanderbilt to-night. When will he be home?"

"Early, if I'm any judge," Mrs. Mason said. "Of late, he avoids his friends—speaks to them as little as possible when he must meet them. And since that horrible affair at the bank—his hair, you know?"

Satan nodded sympathetically. "He looked pretty moth-eaten when I last saw him," he grinned. Suzy snickered, drawing a baleful glare from her mother.

"Anything else?" Satan wanted to know.

"General disagreeableness, absent mindedness, bad manners and the like." Mrs. Mason looked suddenly hopeful. "Are you by any chance a doctor?"

Satan suppressed a chuckle. "After a fashion," he said. "At any rate, I think I can persuade your husband to take a rest for a few days. I wasn't certain that it would be—er—for the best, until I heard your story, Mrs. Mason."

"Oh, he won't rest! Why, he's at the bank at all hours of the day and night."

"He'll rest," Satan repeated softly.

"Well, I'm willing to wager—" A bell rang somewhere in the house, causing Mrs. Mason to lapse into silence. Satan studied her closely, saw a fear grow in her face again.

Suzy jumped to her feet and went to the hall. On the stair landing leading to the next floor, she turned. "Tell him I'm in bed, Mama," she said. "It makes me jittery to see that hair-cut the bandits pinned on him!"

Satan was on his feet. "I hear your servant coming down from upstairs. Please call to him that he needn't bother. I shall answer the door."

Mrs. Mason nodded and went to intercept the houseman. Satan went part of the way downstairs, then stopped and peered at the curtained outer door. He could see but one figure silhouetted against it.

Whistling softly to himself a popular air, he set his hat at a jaunty angle and whipped the door open.

Manse Mason wasn't looking squarely at him. "Ah, Meredith! Nice evening, what?"

"I'll answer that for Meredith," Satan spoke quietly. A blue-black automatic was pointed squarely at the banker's heart. "It's a *very* nice night, Mr. Mason. And if you want it to stay nice, you'll just turn around on those little legs of yours and toddle back down the stoop."

The banker's face was drawn, his eyes fearful. "Who—?" he quavered. "Who—?"

"Are you imitating an owl, or are you trying to ask my name," Satan asked pleasantly as he pushed the man into the vestibule and yanked the door shut. "If you want to know my name—?" He raised his hat and thrust his face close to Mason.

"Satan!" the man croaked. "Oh, God, not Captain Satan?"

"Shut up, or I'll blast you in two right here on your doorstep," Satan snapped. "Down the steps, Mason! Turn left! Up to Fifth Avenue and down to the next street below us. Left, there, again! You'll see a black limousine parked there, motor running. Climb right into it, Mason."

"You can't do this to me," Mason quavered. "You can't!"

Satan stepped close and smashed his gun hard into the man's ribs.

"Get going before I smash every bone in your body! You're going away for a little rest, Mason. And while you're resting, I have a few questions to ask you! Get going! I'll be five paces in back of you—and I couldn't miss at that range!"

CHAPTER 9
BLACK MAGIC

S LIM CAME into the dingy room of the ramshackle cottage that Satan had leased, far out on Long Island. Satan looked up from the evening papers.

"Not a word about the snatch," Satan said. His gray eyes were frankly worried. "Slim, I don't understand it!"

It was as if he were trying to penetrate those masks, trying to find the spy he suspected—the man he was almost certain was hiding behind one of those eye-slitted pieces of cloth. The men lined up against the wall at Satan's right, the candlelight flickering and casting dancing shadows across the hooded figures.

"Bring in the prisoner," Satan ordered solemnly. Slim, standing slightly to one side, moved slowly across the room and through the door. Satan's eyes studied the masked faces intently while he waited.

In a moment the sounds of footsteps came again. Slim's voice, low and solemn, sounded.

"Enter, prisoner."

"Wha—what are you going to do?" a voice quavered.

"Enter, prisoner!"

Manse Mason's head came into view, his eyes round and his mouth loose. He stared at the grim figures that were revealed by the candlelight and tried to back out again. Slim appeared behind him, forced him into the room and shut the door.

Instantly, a strong beam of light sprang into life and fixed on Mason's face. From behind it, Satan watched closely, saw the fear in the man's face. He spoke softly. "Slim."

"Right, Captain?"

Satan handed his lieutenant the photo prints he had taken from the suitcase. "Pin these to the wall near Mason."

The banker blinked in the strong light, his eyes glassy. He looked furtively at the silent crew lined up against the wall near Satan, then turned to watch Slim. He licked his lips nervously when he turned back toward Satan again.

When the photos were pinned in a long row on the wall,

Satan's flash jumped to the one nearest the banker. It showed Mesters, Mason's mysterious friend, and a carload of men. It was one of the shots taken by the photographer in front of the Atlas Bank, the photographer who

had been relieved of his camera by Satan.

"Who is that man?" Satan asked in a low, even voice.

Mason licked his lips again, stirred uneasily. "Wh—which one?" he faltered.

"Who is that man?" Satan repeated. "Don't quibble, Mason. You know which man I mean!"

Mason turned to the print again. "His name is Mesters. He—he's an associate of mine at the bank."

Satan stared at him for a full minute. "He isn't an officer of the bank, Mason. I haven't heard his name mentioned in connection with the bank. Nor in any other matters in finance. What do you mean when you say he's an associate of yours?"

Mason shifted uneasily on his feet. "He's—he's a wealthy Canadian. He's—only lately interested in financial affairs."

"How lately? Just when? Why? How? How did you meet him, and who are his associates?"

Mason's eyes were like a trapped animal's. "He—was just introduced to me, that's all. He had a large sum of money to invest. I'm—I'm advising him on it."

"How large a sum?" Satan persisted. "How did he come by it? Where is it?"

Mason was trying desperately to be convincing. "He's a former mine owner," he said. "His money—he made it mining."

Satan's voice was patient; but inexorable. "What mine? Where? And, how much?"

"I—don't know," Mason faltered.

"You don't know?" Satan smiled grimly, "You, a banker, meet with a man who is a perfect stranger and make him your associate without knowing anything about him?" He laughed. "Maybe a little different sort of persuasion might loosen your tongue, Mason?"

Mason's eyes dropped. "I don't know what mine he owned," he said. "Some Canadian or Western United States property."

"How much money has he?"

Mason moved uneasily again. "I don't know the exact amount. All I know is what he has in the Atlas vaults."

Satan's eyes narrowed. "In the vaults? On deposit, you mean?"

Mason shook his head. "Not on deposit," he said. "He has slightly more than five hundred thousand dollars, earmarked for him, in our vaults."

Satan's eyes reflected the excitement he felt. He sat forward slightly. "Slim," he murmured. "Our friend Mr. Mason must have an interesting story to tell. *And he's going to tell it!* Bring out the branding iron and we'll see if it helps his halting speech any."

Mason trembled; but he didn't speak as he watched Slim go to a closet and return with a wooden-handled piece of metal, the end of which was round and patterned with some device. It was blackened by its many exposures to flame.

Satan took it. "This, Mason," he said, standing and thrusting the end of it into one of the candle flames, "is my own little device to get the truth. It is Satan's Brand! When I'm through with you, I'll have the story—and you'll have maybe twenty imprints of my trademark on your face and body. *If* you live through it," he added significantly.

Mason's eyes dilated with horror as he watched, his nostrils quivered when the smell of scorched metal filled the quiet room. Without looking up, Satan said:

"Slim and Kayo! Bring the prisoner here!"

TWO BLACK-GARBED figures tightened Mason's arms behind his back and forced him forward.

"No, no," the banker moaned. "I've told all I know!"

Satan didn't appear to hear. He held the iron close to his face, nodded his satisfaction to the heat that he felt there. He thrust his hand into the banker's hair and jerked the man's head close to the hot iron.

"I'll tell!" the man gurgled, his eyes crazed with horror. "I'll tell what I know!"

Satan stared at him a long minute, then passed the iron in Slim's direction. "Keep this thing hot, Slim," he said calmly.

"Mason might forget his promise." Then, to the man: "Get over to those pictures and answer my questions!"

Mason sobbed his relief, nearly fell when Slim and Kayo released him. At the wall again, with Satan's flash lighting the prints, Mason said:

"I've told you all I can of Mesters. He has some deals on that require a lot of cash. Secret deals. That's why he doesn't keep his money on deposit. And—"He paused again, his eyes furtive.

"The iron, Slim," Satan said, thrusting out his hand.

Mason cowered. "I'll tell," he babbled. "I—I didn't look into his connections too closely, because he came recommended by the Secretary of the Treasury. I can prove that!"

Satan relaxed and smiled slightly. "Now we're getting someplace," he said. "I have three letters here—letters I took from your safe the other day—that suggested that. What's the Treasury hookup?"

"Mesters has influence," Mason said. "The Treasury is depositing a large amount of gold in our bank. It means much to the bank. It will give us unlimited lending power, for one thing."

Satan frowned. "The Government is making gold deposits with the Atlas Bank?" He studied Mason intently. "Just where does that get you? It still isn't your money, even to lend. Explain what you mean."

Mason shrugged. "It's some idea of Mesters'," he said. "That's all I can say, because I don't know any more."

"What's in it for you?" Satan persisted, his voice unrelenting.

Mason dropped his eyes. "A hundred thousand dollars," he

Satan waited tensely behind the door.

admitted at last. "All I do is to follow orders. For just another week. And the money is mine."

"*Hm.*" Satan considered a moment. "When is this gold transfer coming. Next week?"

Mason nodded. Satan's eyes narrowed. "I begin to see," he said slowly, "why Mesters doesn't want information of your

kidnaping made public. It might block this—move; whatever

it is. And there must be plenty in it for Mesters, or he wouldn't pay you that hundred thousand. But—what?"

Mason didn't answer. Satan pondered for a long moment, then sat up suddenly, his eyes meeting those that peered at him through a mask, one of his crew.

He was recalling Soapy's words about the bank hold-up—the hold-up in which Soapy was to have a part, through the now dead Mugsy the Fish. A new idea was being born in his brain.

"How much of a gold shipment is this?" he asked at last.

"Five million dollars," Mason said.

Satan considered. The thing was preposterous… that thing he had thought of. You couldn't walk off with five millions in gold, not under the noses of police and government officials. You couldn't do it under the eyes of ordinary citizens, even. The weight of the stuff alone….

He shook his head in perplexity. "There's something very odd about this whole set-up," he said finally. "Just what, I don't know. But I'll know about it before I'm through!

"Now—that carload of men to whom Mesters is talking?" he pursued. "Who are they?"

Mason turned his eyes to the print. "I never saw them before. I'm not lying."

Satan turned to his men. "Take a look. Ever see any of that crowd before?"

One by one, the men inspected the photo in question. One by one, each shook his head. "All right," Satan said. "Now—the next photo. Know any of those men?"

Mason didn't. Nor did any of the others… until Soapy had his look.

"Cap'n," the diminutive Soapy exclaimed, "I know two of these men. The ones standing here next to Mesters! One of 'em is Lobo Louie, a Western trigger man. The other one is 'Rowdy Bob' Cash, a 'Frisco ex-pug. I haven't seen either one of them in more than a year."

"Gangsters?"

"Yep," Soapy said. "Used to work for Joie Maganni. You know? The guy who disappeared when the G-men went after him as head of that big snatch ring? The kidnap gang?"

Satan nodded. Joe Maganni had terrorized the country west of the Mississippi with his daring kidnaps, had piled up a fortune and then had vanished utterly. He turned to Mason.

"And you don't know those men either?"

Mason shook his head. "Mesters has some—er—bodyguards, who look after him," he said. "I've seen some of them. But I don't know those men."

Satan signed to Slim to take the photos down again. "All right, Mason. Now—these letters, addressed to you by the Treasury." He passed them to Slim to show Mason, then got them back again.

"Two of them relate to some investment that you evidently discussed with the Treasury Department—a Foreign investment, evidently, since it states that the Department is not in favor of the matter because of 'neutrality laws.' Just what is this about?"

Mason's eyes went shifty again. "I—er—it relates to a Spanish holding company. That's Mesters' idea, too."

"Oh," Satan's face lighted up. "Now we're getting down to something, I think! Your bank is made a gold depository for the Treasury? And you have a deal on foot to make a heavy investment in some Spanish holding company?"

Mason nodded. Satan's eyes bored into him before he took up the last of the three letters. "And just what happened to make the Treasury do an about face and write this?" He read: " 'Carry out matters as decided in our recent meeting?' What does that mean?"

Mason's eyes darted around the tense group, then came back to Satan.

"It means," he said with apparent reluctance, "that the Treasury has put the okay on Mesters' deal."

Satan stared at the man, then shook his head slowly.

"There's some sort of black magic at work," he said, "when the Treasury will do an about face on a decision like this—when Government officials will appoint a bank as a gold depository for no apparent reason, for no apparent gain on anyone's part—

"And when the head of the Atlas Bank can disappear under strange circumstances without one word appearing in print about it! Well, Mason, I intend to find out what it's all about!"

He turned to Slim. "Take the prisoner back," he said slowly. "Put him under guard of two men. Send the rest of the boys out to complete their unfinished business—or whatever there is of it. As for myself—I'm going to pay the bank a visit and see what goes on in Mason's absence! Get me that bunch of keys we took from him."

CHAPTER 10
INTO THIN AIR

KAYO TOOLED the big car slowly along darkened downtown Broadway. At Wall Street, a block south of the Atlas Bank, Satan spied a furtive shadow in a doorway.

"Turn right here, Kayo," he called from where he was slouched in the rear seat. "Skirt east of the bank and come back down from the other way. There's a lookout posted there."

"I see him, Cap'n," Kayo said, turning the wheel. "If I don't miss my guess, you'll have one on every corner."

Kayo proved to be right. There was a shadow lurking in a doorway at each corner beyond the bank block. As they came south on Broadway again, Satan said, "Circle back around the other way, Kayo. I'll get down and walk back. Meantime, you stop near the guard down by Wall Street. Get him into conversation, if you can. Then drive up slowly toward the next man. I'll do the rest."

Kayo nodded. Satan could see by the street light that his face was tense, slightly pale. It was a dangerous spot, but Satan was determined to go through with it. Out of view of the bank, he opened the door of the car and dropped from the running board while the auto was still in motion.

He came close to the building line and sped a block down, then crossed back to Broadway. Kayo's lights showed as he rounded the corner above, at a snail's pace. The lights came close to the curb, stopped. The figure came out from the shadows, stood close to the car. Satan made the far building line in a jump, came fast toward the upper corner.

The man on watch there was standing with his back to him, talking to Kayo. Satan saw his hand in his pocket, went more carefully. He gained the far side of the street, ducked into the doorway the man had quit and waved a signal to Kayo.

The gears of the car meshed and Satan heard Kayo call: "Thanks. It's tough bein' a stranger in this town. Hard to find your way around."

The guard stood staring after the departed car, then came slowly back to his lookout post. He didn't see Satan until the clubbed gun was inches from his head… and then it was too late.

There was a dull thud; then Satan caught the man in his arms and lowered him into the dark shadows of the doorway. He played a flash on the man's face, then thrust his hand into one pocket after another of the guard's clothes. He stiffened when his hand contacted a bit of metal. It was a badge.

"A Treasury investigator," he muttered, staring at the thing.

But he remembered Kayo… who would be at the next corner… and his own determination to get into that bank. He helped himself to the man's gun, shoved the badge into his own pocket, slid out of the doorway and looked up the avenue.

Kayo's lights were showing where the car was stopped two blocks up. Satan went rapidly up the building line, ducked for a moment when he saw the man up the street turn his head. He came out again when the man turned back to Kayo. In another moment he was opposite the private entrance to the big institution.

He tried five keys from Mason's ring before he found the right one. Then he pushed the door open quickly and stepped inside. Noiselessly, he shut the door after him. He stood in the dark of the place, his eyes going round. Through a glass door in front of him he could see a light burning in the bank, could see the doors of the great vault that took up a portion of one of the walls. To the left, where Manse Mason's private office was, a light shone through frosted glass.

"There's someone there," Satan murmured with a tightening of his breathing. "And that someone is… Mesters!"

He was taking his first step in that direction when a voice sounded at his side.

"Don't make one move—you! We've been expecting you, but you've kept us waiting a long time!" The voice said.

Satan slid his eyes around, saw a shadowy figure in the uniform of a special guard standing a few feet away, a figure whose out-thrust hand held an ugly automatic.

FOR PERHAPS one minute, Satan stood very still. Then he forced a low, easy laugh.

"Put that thing up, you fool," he said. "I'm one of the Government guards. From outside." He waited breathlessly to see if it would work. The 'Special' was still wary. "I want to tell Mr. Mesters that there's an automobile fooling around outside."

Inwardly, he was wondering at this man's words… 'We've been expecting you'… while he watched the man's reactions.

The guard stirred. "Oh," he said. "I saw that 'bus tooling up the line." But his eyes were still doubtful. "You're a G-man?"

Satan nodded. "Want to see my badge?" He started a hand to his pocket; but held it rigid at the guard's move.

"Quit that!" the man snarled. "What pocket's it in? I'll have a look for myself."

"Right hand pocket of my coat. With my gun," Satan told him.

The guard jammed the muzzle of the automatic into Satan's ribs while he thrust his other hand into the pocket. He pulled out the gun, transferred it to his pocket. "I'll just hang on to this a minute," he said meaningly. Then he yanked the badge out, cocked his head while he held it close and peered.

In that second, Satan slid his hand under the lapel of his jacket and brought out a gun; his own gun. The guard, reassured that he had Satan's weapon when he pocketed the arm that had been taken from the unconscious G-man, was relaxed.

Satan whipped the thing in a vicious arc to the guard's jaw, grabbed with his other hand for the gun the man held. The fellow's knees crumpled. But he fought to grab Satan, to hold himself up. The gun went up and down again with a sickening *thwack* and the guard slid into unconsciousness.

Satan knew he'd have to work fast, to find out who was in that office and what was going on. The presence of the G-man outside bewildered him. He couldn't understand the connection between the mysterious Mesters and the G-men who represented the Treasury Department.

But he knew in his own heart that he had gone too far to

turn back now, and that he wouldn't want to quit this mysterious adventure if he could.

He made his way quickly and noiselessly across the great floor of the bank, stood for a moment outside the door of the private hall that led to Mason's office. No sound came. He opened the door, slid into the hall on the other side. Just a step from the door to Mason's anteroom, he stopped.

Voices came to him from the other side… voices that he knew were coming from Mason's office. When he was sure that no one was in the anteroom, he pushed that door open quietly, stepped inside. He crossed to the far door.

Someone was speaking… talking in a low, steady voice.

"…The gold shipment will be pushed up to the day after tomorrow," that voice was saying. "We can't risk Satan's meddling any longer. Nothing can stop us now. We have the necessary permits for the removal of the gold, in case we're stopped, and they are ready to be signed by Secretary of the Treasury Pettiman."

Satan realized, with a start of excitement, that it was Mesters speaking… that one of the biggest swindles in history was about to be enacted.

Another voice chimed in. "You're sure there'll be no slip up?"

"There can't be," Mesters answered positively. "Ten million will be a small take before I'm through with this game. This country is about to go haywire."

The other voice cut in. "You're sure the President won't gum the whole thing up the last minute? He could, you know."

A hard laugh sounded. "The President," Mesters said in a

voice that was suddenly harsh, "won't be around to stop anything! The President slides tomorrow night... vanishes into thin air!"

Satan gasped with the stunning force of the thing. The President—the President of the United States! But—*vanish?* He wondered if his senses weren't tricking him... wondered if he had gone mad, suddenly, was hearing things that were never being said... was doing things that he only imagined he was doing.

Then, suddenly, it occurred to him that it was this other man who was mad... that it was Mesters who was insane, crazed by a lust for wealth and power, stopping at nothing in this wild scheme to add to his already ample wealth. In some way, this remarkable maniac was getting a death grip on the United States Government, had already gotten that grip, if the events which were being discussed on the other side of that door were true.

His wildly racing thoughts were interrupted by the ringing of the telephone inside Mason's office. Mesters had answered it... was speaking.

"What?... Who?... Yes, yes; go ahead...."

Satan's heart skipped a great beat at the next words.

"...You're with Mason now? On Long Island? No, no. Tell him to come right here, to the bank, when he gets loose. But tell him to get loose in his own way. *Do you understand what I mean?*"

Satan's senses reeled. A telephone call from someone who said that he was with Mason? He wondered for a minute if he were being tricked by Mesters, if Mesters in some way knew that he, Satan, was hidden in that outside room, was now laying a trap for him to fall into.

But the next words convinced him he was wrong in this.

"…Did Mason spill anything about me? Only that I was a mining man, eh?" Mesters laughed aloud. "Where's Satan now?" was his next question. Then: *"What?* On his way here? *To the bank?* I've been hoping for that!"

Satan's mind raced through the meaning of this call. Someone in his own crew was a traitor—someone who had been in on that star chamber session with Mason—was telephoning to Mesters, reporting the details of the questioning, reporting… *Mason's escape!*

"Of course it's Mason's escape," Satan thought as his mind flashed over the thing. "But—how?"

He was turning to the door when Mesters' next words came to him.

"…But he didn't tell him I was Joie Maganni? You're sure?…"

Satan's astonishment was so great that he stood rooted to the spot, his face wearing the blank expression of a sleep walker, dazed so that he was powerless to move.

"Joie Maganni!" he breathed. "But—he *isn't.* Or, it isn't Mesters who is in there!" But he knew it was Mesters' voice.

Satan had never met Maganni in person, but recalled well enough the published photos of the notorious kidnaper. And he knew that Mesters looked no more like Maganni than he, Satan, did.

The voice cut in on his thought, spurred him to action.

"…I'll be ready for Satan when he gets here," Mesters was

saying. "I'll fix him so he won't meddle with my affairs any more… the human devil!"

Satan had things to do…. He had to get outside, get back to the Long Island retreat, to find if what he had heard was true … though he couldn't credit what his own ears had heard.

"That," Satan thought as he hurriedly went out of the ante-room and through the hall. "That and stop this crazy man—Mesters or Maganni or whoever he is—from staging the greatest snatch of all times: the President of the United States!"

ON THE street outside, Satan blew three shrill, whistling blasts through his teeth, then dodged back into the doorway. He could hear a motor race to sudden life somewhere nearby, could hear gears ripping into high speed.

Broadway was deserted. Up one block, a guard stepped out from his hiding as the car screamed around a corner on two wheels. Satan jumped out and sped into the street.

The door of the car swung open under Kayo's hand and Satan scrambled in. "Full speed away," he snapped. "Don't stop for anything. Back to Long Island!"

"Right, Cap'n," Kayo clipped as the car shot into speed again.

From down the street sounded the sudden crash of an automatic. Two bullets spanged into the rear of the fleeing auto.

CHAPTER 11
GUTS AND GUNS

THE CAR sped through the darkness of Long Island under the smoothly expert handling of Kayo. In the rear seat, Satan forced himself to concentrate on what he had heard at the bank, though it took Spartan effort.

Time and again, his thoughts leaped to the Long Island house, wondering what he would find there.... But he knew that there must be some truth in what was said in Mason's office.

For one thing, he knew that when Mason had been threatened with torture that his words came somewhat close to the truth.

And it brought into evidence again the fact that somewhere in the crew was a spy, a renegade. Satan wondered if it wouldn't be better to face the issue squarely, to trace the suspected spy through fingerprints.

But he decided against it. "If Mason's gone," he realized, "the spy has probably gone with him. If he hasn't—" he smiled grimly, "I'll let him play along with us. He's bound to give himself away before this thing is over. And he's my only contact with the mob at the moment. He and Mesters, Maganni, or whatever the rat's real name happens to be."

Kayo slowed as they came to the slightly used road leading to the hideout. When he turned and the outline of the house down the lane came into view, Satan's heart beat faster. He wondered—

There were lights in every room of that house. Kayo grunted.

"Hey, Cap'n! Look. I thought the boys were supposed to keep the place dark?"

"Step on it," Satan growled. He slid out of the car when the brakes screeched to a stop, drew his gun and signaled Kayo to follow.

The door was closed, but unlocked. Satan pushed it open and then stood back, listening. Utter silence greeted him from inside.

"Slim?" he called, after a moment.

No answer.

Satan moved carefully inside, Kayo following and closing the door. Satan led the way upstairs, his eyes alert and his ears cocked. He stopped in the hall, his eyes on the door behind which Mason had been locked. He tried the knob and found it still closed.

But he started when a voice called from within: "Hey! Let me out, whoever you are!"

It wasn't the voice of the banker Mason. Satan blinked. "Stand guard here," he directed Kayo. He went into his own room, the room where the meeting had been held. Everything was in disorder. Satan saw at a glance that his suitcase had been rifled, that the photos and the letters he had purloined were missing... all but one photo—a close-up of the man, Mesters, which the raider had evidently dropped in his haste.

From the closet in the corner came a muffled sound, as of someone struggling, ineffectually, to get out. Satan crossed with quick strides and jerked open the door. There, in a huddle on the floor, bound hand and foot, and gagged, were Slim... and Soapy... and Frenchy.

Soapy was still. Slim had suffered a deep gash over one eye. Frenchy wore a lump the size of an egg on his chin; but he was struggling to get loose. It was he who was making the commotion and had worked his bonds all but off. With Kayo's help, Satan cut their ropes and helped them out of the closet. Slim's eyes were ashamed and avoided Satan's.

"Sorry, Captain," he muttered. "They got us... in some way."

"I knew that an hour ago," Satan said slowly. His eyes were watchful when he added, "Someone... *someone* telephoned that Mason was free!"

But there was nothing other than astonishment in the faces of the men who stared back at him. After a moment, Satan spoke again.

"Who's in that room? How did they get to you men?"

"I was in here," Slim spoke first. "I heard some sort of noise outside and poked my head out. The next thing I knew the lights went out, I was in that closet when I woke up, Captain."

"Slugged," Satan nodded. He turned to Frenchy and Soapy. "You two were on guard, eh?"

Frenchy nodded. "Yeah. Mason was asking for water, so I went downstairs to draw a pitcher of it for him. While I was running the tap, someone stuck a gun on me and cracked me with a blackjack. I put up a fight and got another poke in the jaw with the billy. I never did see who it was, Cap'n."

Satan's eyes were hard. "You, Soapy?"

The little man was sheepish. "I heard Frenchy coming up with the water. At least, I thought it was Frenchy. Then someone put the bee on me an' I come to in the closet, Cap'n."

"Nice work," Satan commented acidly. "Three smart lads let

a man crawl up on them and fix their wagon!" His eyes shifted to the hall door. "Who's in that room now?"

The three looked at him with round eyes. "Huh? Is someone in there?" Slim asked.

"Come on," Satan said, leading the way.

Slim took a key from his pocket, stared at it in astonishment. "For the love of—? I never thought I'd find this here! I wonder—?"

He slid the key into the lock, turned it. And the four of them stood staring at a man who came towards them, his face pale with rage, a water-pitcher held in his hand in a defensive attitude, spilling fluid to the floor.

No florid faced man, this... though he was portly, somewhat, as Mason had been. Dark eyed, red haired, white of face, instead of blue eyed, gray haired, red faced.

"Who are you?" Satan asked.

"Who are you?" the stranger snapped. "What's the idea of grabbing me off the road outside and stuffing me in here? Where are my clothes?"

Slim looked. "He's got Mason's suit on," he said. "Same tie, too."

Satan cut him off. "What's your story, you? Cut the questioning and answer mine."

The stranger was puzzled. "Why—I thought you might know," he said. "I was driving along the road near here when a man came up, waved to me to stop, then jammed a gun into my ribs. He made me drive here, then forced me to change clothes with him. After that he locked me in. That's all I can tell you about it." He looked hopeful. "Are you a policeman?" the stranger asked.

Satan shook his head. "Never mind what I am. What did this man look like—the one who stuck you up?"

The red headed one squinted. "About my size, I judge. Gray haired, and sort of red faced. And blue eyes, I think."

Satan blinked and stared at Slim. "Mason himself," he said. To the man again: "Who are you?"

"Harman Jenkins," the man said promptly. "I'm in the advertising business, and live at Centre Moriches." He frowned suddenly. "That other mug took my car, didn't he?"

Satan shrugged. "I can't help that. But—you'll have to get out of here."

"*Will* I?" the man laughed suddenly. "Say, I'll forget about the car and the rest of it if I can just get away from here. When do I go?"

"Right away," Satan said grimly. "I'll have you dropped at the railroad station, give you some money to get home." He turned:

"Kayo! Take this man to the station. And come right back. We're pulling out of here right away! Slim; search him for anything suspicious."

With the strange redhead gone with the driver, Satan started to speak, then stopped. He motioned Slim to follow him into his room.

Once inside, Satan shook his head sadly. "One of the boys has turned crooked on us, Slim."

The lieutenant shrugged. "Looks like it," he admitted. "I can make a pretty close guess, I think."

"I don't want any guessing," Satan said. "I want to *know!* And when I do!" Slim shuddered at the savage look that came into those gray eyes.

Swiftly, Satan told him of the events of the night. When he came to the part about Maganni, Slim stared, dumfounded. "But Maganni doesn't look anything like the man you describe as Mesters," he protested.

Satan nodded. He was thinking. "Whatever the game was up to now, Slim," he said soberly, "it's changed. I came into this thing to track down a smart gang, to knock them off for whatever they have. But it's different, now. The life of the President of the United States is in danger. The life of the President and the future of the country, maybe. With what is going on in Washington to-day, the disappearance of the President would just about stand the nation on its head—bring revolution—ruin!"

Slim stared. "What's on the program now, Captain?" he wanted to know.

"We're going to Washington," Satan said. "Just you and I, and Kayo. I'm going to stop this gang if it's the last thing I do."

"I'm afraid it might be the last thing you do at that," Slim murmured as he turned away.

ONCE IN the national capital, Satan made for the seclusion of a room in a small hotel and sat for some time with Slim. The slender man maintained a long silence while his chief speculated on events.

"Slim," Satan said at last, "here's what gets me: How am I going to warn the President, to make him aware of his danger? I can't get to him personally, can I—with the G-men after me?

108

And if I write, my letter would be put in the 'crank file'... the place where the communications of every crack-pot who writes the President are kept."

"Telephone him," Slim suggested.

"And have the call traced, to bring the G-men down on us? I can't do that."

Slim looked doubtful when he offered another suggestion. "How about a disguise? If you could get up a decent one, now—?"

"Not with the close scrutiny you'd get going into the White House," Satan disagreed. "A disguise might get by with a few people, but...." His voice trailed off into silence, but his eyes were full of things as they stared at his lieutenant.

"Slim," he said in a tense voice, "I've seen a few disguises in my time. Some were good. But—have you ever seen a disguise where the color of a man's eyes could be changed?"

Slim snorted. "Listen, Captain—it's hard enough to get the texture of the skin right. You know that. A wig can be picked out by a smart eye. And hair dye shows after the hair grows a bit. But as for changing the color of a man's eyes—"

Satan nodded. "Yes. But there are a few things that have me puzzled about this case. Mesters says that he is Maganni—yet he works right under the noses of the G-men and the police. Remember the pictures?"

Slim disagreed. "You *think* he said it, Captain. You didn't see him, remember."

Satan's eyes were narrowed. "As well as we know Sledge— knew him, rather—a man shows up in his place at one of our meetings. That man is identified by fingerprints as a man named

Martin. Yet he doesn't answer Martin's description. How about that?"

Slim couldn't answer it. His face was frankly puzzled.

"We lock Mason in a room, open it and find a stranger there in his place." Excitement shone in Satan's face now, and he sat tensed. "But the man in his place is about the same size, isn't he? He is wearing Mason's clothes, isn't he?" He paused suddenly, his eyes going wide.

"Slim!" He jumped to his feet. "What fools we are! Do you remember, Frenchy was bringing him a pitcher of water when he was jumped?" Slim stared. "Yes, Captain. But—?"

Satan's eyes were hard. "The man in that room had a water pitcher in his hand—and water was sloshing to the floor from it!"

"Oh, my God," Slim breathed. "So—the water pitcher that Frenchy was bringing him got to that room, somehow?"

"Right. And if Frenchy was jumped when he was drawing the water, how did the man who attacked him know that Mason, locked in that room, wanted water? It must have been because he needed water—had to have the water, for some reason, in order to escape!"

Slim's eyes had gone narrow. "It could mean that, Cap'n. Or it could mean something else." His face was bleak when he added, "It could be—"

But Satan wasn't listening. "Before we got rid of the stranger, did you frisk him? You searched him?"

Slim nodded. "Didn't find anything but some small, broken

bits of glass, Captain. In a vestpocket. I figured they came from his watch. Broke it, maybe."

Satan's eyes were keen. "And you checked your guess with his watch? With Mason's watch?"

Slim's eyes were miserable. "I remember, Captain—that the watch was not broken. I let it go with the stranger, figuring we didn't want the thing found on us, in case anything went wrong."

Satan's eyes were calculating. "Then, that glass must have been from something that has a lot to do with the mysterious disappearance of Mason. But—what could it have been—what could those broken bits of glass mean?"

Slim sat silent. Satan's face grew more serious, more lined, as he pursued some reasoning that he was struggling with. He looked up at last, excitement shining in his eyes.

"Slim—I've seen some pretty big things in my time, some pretty big frauds and 'fixes.' But I think we're up against something now so big that it's breath-taking. Slim—just how good do you think a man could make a disguise, a *changeable* disguise?"

Slim, baffled, sat silent. Satan got to his feet after a few minutes.

"I have a friend in Washington whose father is an expert in some matters that interest me. I'm going to pay him a call, Slim—see if he can't tell me to what degree a man who isn't Manse Mason could *look* like Mason… and fool people enough to get away with it!"

THIRTY MINUTES later, Satan stood in the vestibule of the address on N Street to which the property of the Sarno household had been directed. He was surprised at the great size of the house, puzzled at the shabbiness of the street on which it was situated.

He waited some time after the bell had sounded in the interior of the house. He was disappointed when there was no answer.

"Must be out," he conjectured.

But as he went down the steps to the street again, he was puzzled to see the curtain behind the closed window on the first floor tremble, as if someone had just let it back into place, hurriedly… someone who had been watching.

He retraced his steps and rang again; this time, twice, as if to let the occupants know that their presence inside was known to him. He wasn't surprised to hear footsteps this time, to have the door opened slightly and a surly, scowling face peer out at him through the slight crack.

Satan smiled disarmingly when he saw the signs. "Don't want to let me in, eh?" he guessed. He walked as if to speak confidentially, tripped purposely on the doormat and fell heavily against the door.

"Sorry," he grinned at the small, hard faced man holding the door. He pushed the last foot of the way in. "Tripped over the mat. Is Miss Sarno at home?"

"No; she isn't," the surly little man answered. "Now, if you'll just go out—"

"When is she expected?" Satan asked pleasantly. His eyes roved over the dark hall, travelled up the long stairs, slid back to the door at his right. Was he mistaken, he wondered, or was there some slight disturbance there?—like someone struggling…?

"She isn't expected," the man snapped. "Now, I've got to get back to my work. If you'll step out again—"

Someone *was* at that door… someone who said, "Let *go* of me, I tell you!" And the door was thrust open suddenly.

Marianne Sarno stood there, her face flushed, eyes flashing, her hair awry. Satan had a glimpse of a large woman stepping hastily out of sight. But he acted as if he had noticed nothing.

"Hello," he said. "Just passing through the city, so I dropped in to call. How are you?"

Marianne's eyes were desperately glad to see him. "I'm so glad you came!" She turned, obviously struggling for composure; as if she feared something, yet was hoping frantically for the best.

"This is a friend of mine from New York, Martha," she said to the other woman. "I'll talk to him a few minutes. In here… if you don't mind."

The coarse face of the woman called Martha appeared out of the gloom beyond the door, large and truculent, and somewhat baffled. Her eyes met with those of the little man who had let Satan in. Satan sensed rather than saw a signal pass between the two; a command, he suspected. Then the big woman grinned toothily.

"All right, dearie," she simpered. "But not for long, mind! You mustn't get overtired!"

Satan blinked his astonishment; but he stepped inside the room. Marianne pushed the door shut resolutely… but she stood listening a moment, as if wondering if it would be permitted. After a moment, she signed to Satan to sit in a chair by the farthest wall from the door. She slipped into the one next to him.

"I don't know who you are," she whispered. "But—somehow—I trust you. I'm not ill; although these dreadful people make out I am."

"Who are they?" Satan asked, his eyes puzzled. "How about your father? Why does he permit this?"

"Oh, Dad is so peculiar," Marianne said. "I rarely see him at all; now that we are in Washington. These people are supposed to be servants. They act more like guards."

"But, why guards?" Satan asked, perplexed. He had come to talk with Sarno, but his mind was occupied with the strange behavior of the people in this house. For a moment, he wondered if Sarno were mad, if, indeed, both Sarnos—father and daughter—weren't a bit touched in the head.

But the girl's clear, honest eyes dismissed that thought.

"I wish I could tell you about—things," she said, after another anxious glance at the door. "But father made me promise not to breathe a word of what I see, or hear."

Satan considered. "I don't suppose your father can spare much time," he said. "But I'd like to see him. On a matter of great importance."

Marianne shook her head. "He won't see anyone," she said, adding bitterly. "Not even me." Her eyes were puzzled. "But, why on earth would you want to see father?"

Satan shrugged. "I just wanted to ask him something about

hair and skin and eyes," he said. "I wanted to know to what degree it is possible for one man to impersonate another. A man in the public eye, I mean."

Marianne's eyes had gone wide as he posed his problem. Now her gaze was stricken, her hand going to her mouth.

"Oh!" she breathed. "You—you aren't one of the men threatening the—?" She stopped, her eyes going to the hall door. The bell had sounded for the outside door.

Satan frowned. What did Marianne mean by " 'You're not one of the men threatening—?'" Threatening *whom?* And why did the question of disguise, of double identity, strike such terror to her?

Someone in the hall had opened the door, and heavy footsteps were coming down the stairs from the floor above. There was a heavy, jovial voice raised in greeting… then another voice, vaguely familiar, answering.

The heavy voice asked, "What's the news? It's a nuisance being without a telephone. But—you know the reasons!"

The vaguely familiar voice: "So you got the Big Shot, did you?"

"Yes. This morning."

The familiar voice was now *definitely* familiar. "Well—you'd better work fast. Satan's in Washington!"

"What?" Then a harsh laugh. "He's too late. The gold has been shipped, and I'm on my way to see that everything works smoothly."

Satan had started to his feet at the mention of his name. But now Marianne was holding out a warning hand. "Be quiet! That's Coulter Kane, President of the United States!"

"What?" Satan all but shouted. His mind was awhirl. Why was the President talking about *him?* And… that other voice… was it—? could it be—?

There was a sudden silence outside, a silence as of people put on their guard, of people suspicious. The servants must have told those two, by this time, of the stranger in their midst.

Satan slid to his feet and started on tiptoe for the far end of the room.

But suddenly the door was flung back on its hinges.

"Satan!" a voice snarled. A man was in the doorway, hand streaking for his hip. But Satan was faster. His automatic was in his hand as quick as he could flick the lapel of his coat.

"Frenchy," Satan murmured as he pulled the trigger.

CHAPTER 12
THE DEVIL HAS A DOUBLE

THE TRAITOR of Satan's Crew staggered under the force of the bullet, then caught himself with a hand on the wall and steadied. His own gun crashed twice, the second bullet ripping through Satan's right sleeve and searing his arm.

Carefully, Satan aimed and fired again, the roar of the gun shattering the air of the room. Frenchy dropped his gun and a bloody smear crept over his smashed hand. His left struggled feebly toward his other pocket.

His face grim as Death, Satan fired still another shot. Frenchy dropped to his knees, his other hand broken by Satan's careful aim. Marianne screamed when another figure, large, faultlessly dressed, good looking with his wavy, dark hair and flashing brown eyes, stepped through the door and whipped a weapon into view.

Satan paused a moment when he saw who it was—Coulter Kane, President of the United States!

"Drop that gun," he snapped, his voice begging for understanding. "There's some sort of plot afoot here, Mr. President. You're in with the wrong crowd! *Drop it!*"

But Kane whipped the weapon up and fired, blindly, wildly. With a groan of impotent rage, Satan sighed carefully again… and fired! The President was spun half around by the force of the bullet that caught him high on his shoulder.

Before the man could recover himself, Satan stepped forward swiftly and brought the butt of his gun down on Kane's head in a crashing blow. The President fell.

Marianne screamed again, came at Satan like a Fury. "You—you've shot the President!" she choked, flailing at Satan with both hands. But Satan pushed her away brusquely and bent over.

"He'll live," he said grimly, straightening. He looked down the hall. "Where have that man and woman gone?"

At a noise from below stairs, he stared at Marianne a moment. "I can't explain now," he said, his eyes desperate. "But if you or anyone else stops me now, God knows what will happen to the country!"

"You've shot the President," Marianne whispered, her eyes wide with the horror of the thing. *"You've shot the President!"*

Satan shook her roughly. "Snap out of it! Is there a downstairs front exit?"

"No," the girl gasped. "It's been closed with a steel wall. And father has the only key to the rear exit, below. You—can't get to him. He's locked in his workroom every day."

Satan stared, then turned and dropped to his knees beside Frenchy. One look told him that the man was dying, had been fatally struck by that first bullet. The man opened his eyes as Satan looked. He licked his blood flecked lips and smiled tightly.

"Satan," he whispered. "Satan, you human devil, you've done me in!"

Satan eased the man's head with a pillow from a chair. He looked at him a vengeful second, then he softened, spoke gently.

"Frenchy, why did you do it?"

Frenchy looked with glazed eyes for a second, then closed his lids. "I couldn't get out of it, Cap'n. I got mixed up with the Joie Maganni mob a year ago. I knew they would kill me if I tried to back out."

"So you tried to kill me?" Satan asked.

Frenchy breathed with difficulty now. "Yes," he said. "But I was afraid to tip them off to too much. I thought—well, I know you, Satan," he smiled slightly. "I was afraid you would get wise, would get me."

Satan thought for a moment, his ears alert for sounds from below. Then he turned to his former trustee. "Frenchy," he said, "you did a pretty good job out there on Long Island when you sprung Mason. But you made one mistake. You said you were getting a pitcher of water for Mason downstairs when you were slugged. Nevertheless, *that water was upstairs when we found the redhead!* I knew then that you were lying. That either you had brought the.water upstairs yourself when you were supposed to be knocked out, or else somebody else did. And how would anybody else know that Mason wanted water? That was the giveaway, Frenchy."

Frenchy nodded. His eyes were filming, growing heavy. There wouldn't be much more of life for Frenchy now. So Satan spoke rapidly. "And that redhead, Frenchy—that was the same fellow who appeared as Mason at the meeting, wasn't it? But who and where is the real Mason? How did you change the man so cleverly, so completely?"

Frenchy's eyes came alive a bit. He shifted them to Marianne. "I—guess you'll know soon enough," he whispered.

Satan bent closer, his mind more certain now. "What about King Cal Merrill?" he said, his mouth close to Frenchy's ear, "And how did Mason change the color of his eyes from blue to black?"

Frenchy smiled slowly. His voice was weaker... weaker. "You know too much already," he whispered. "But—Maganni has the signals set on you this time. He can't lose. The set-up is too perfect. You're—you're a genius, Satan. But you came in too late to save... anything."

He stopped talking; and Satan knew that Frenchy would never speak again.

He rose and turned to the girl. "Well? Are you going to string with me? Will you trust me—just for a little?"

Marianne shook her head, her eyes half crazed. "I guess I'm crazy," she said weakly. "But—I trust you. I think you're trying to be straight, anyway."

"Come on," he said grimly, starting for the stairs.

AT THE head of the stair well, Satan stopped her. His eyes were intent on the dark below; but he stood cautiously concealed.

"Tell me as quickly as you can what's been going on here," he said in a low voice. *"All* of it. Leave out nothing!"

"I told you about father's new formula experiments?" she said. "Well—it seems a man came to dad in New York, told him of a gigantic plot to kill Coulter Kane and some other big men. Dad had worked out two things that they wanted…. A face paint that can be put on in liquid form and is practically identical with skin texture, and a new type of hair dye."

"What?" Satan asked. He stared at her, incredulous. "But— what do you mean by a 'liquid skin'? I don't understand?"

"Make-up," Marianne said. "You can get a man who looks very much like another and model his features. But until father's discovery, it was always bound to show at close range, looked artificial."

"Now they can shape noses, chins, eyebrows, even? And do a perfect job, one impossible to detect?"

"Yes," Marianne said. "That was the big secret. That and the hair dye. The dye is made of a chemical that seals the hair in the pores of the scalp… makes it so it won't grow while the dye is in it. In that way the natural color will never show. The dye is permanently there unless removed with a special powder, a solvent, mixed with water."

"The pitcher," Satan said slowly. "That's what did the trick, all right. Frenchy slugged Soapy and Slim, then brought Mason a pitcher of water and passed him the powder. Then he locked him in again to confuse us, and to get us from the hideout!"

"I don't understand what this is all about," Marianne complained.

"I can't explain now," Satan said, his eyes going back to that door below. "But—how about eyes? How can you change the color of eyes?"

Marianne shook her head, a slow smile coming over her face. "You can't do that," she said. "Not even father could do a thing like that."

"I wonder?" Satan murmured. Then: "Is your father down there?"

"Yes."

"Then I've got to go down. I must see him, talk with him."

"But, those other two?" Marianne whispered. "That horrible little man and the filthy woman who stood guard over me? What is it all about—Satan?"

Satan grinned at her hesitant use of his name. "I can't tell you now," he said. He looked around and spied a chair halfway down the hall. He got it and brought it back, made steps with his feet as a man would going down stairs.

Then, with a yell, he let the chair go... to sound like a man rushing that closed door. For several seconds, there was nothing but the bumping of the chair on the bare boards. Then the door below snapped open and streaks of orange flame flashed out.

Satan shot accurately, deliberately. There was a scream, then a thud as the defender below slumped to the floor, Satan heard the sound of running feet below. "Come on," he snapped. "I got one—but the other's running back in the house, below."

"Toward father's room," Marianne murmured fearfully as she followed him.

AT THE foot of the stairs, Satan paused only long enough to flash a light on the fallen form. It was the woman! The big woman who had guarded Marianne. He peered closer, put out a hand and snatched the wig off 'her' head.

"Just as I suspected," he said grimly. "A man dressed up as a woman!"

He straightened at a hammering that came from down the hall.

"Open up, Professor," a voice called. "Hurry! It's important!"

"No," Marianne screamed, pushing to get past Satan. "No, Dad! No!"

Satan sprang into action when he heard a querulous reply, then the sound of a bolt being drawn. He sped down a short hall, came into a blind. He turned, puzzled.

"It's a false panel," Marianne whimpered. "Oh, hurry, Satan. Hurry!"

Satan threw his weight against the panel, once, twice. It gave with a splintering crash. He reached in and turned the catch on the inside. Ahead of him, framed in the doorway, his face peering out of a brightly lighted room, was Professor Sarno.

The little man that had admitted Satan was trying to push past him. Satan snapped, "Hold it, you! Up with your hands or I'll shoot!"

The professor stared a moment, puzzled. Then he attempted to thrust the intruder out again. But the little man was desperate. He made an attempt to wrestle the professor clear, then snarled when he saw Satan closing in.

"You bungling old idiot," he screamed. "Get back and shut this door!"

"You—get—out!" Professor Sarno panted.

And then it happened.

The man threw an agonized look at Satan, tried to raise his weapon clear and fire. But Sarno's body was in his way. There was a roar as the heavy automatic discharged squarely into Sarno's stomach. The man slipped to the floor without a sound.

Satan ripped two shots from his hip and the little gangster staggered wildly a moment before he, too, crumpled. Behind Satan, Marianne moaned and pushed her way forward.

SATAN STOOD in silence a moment, then slowly eased past Marianne. The girl was on her knees, trying to raise her father's head—a head that Satan knew was already lifeless.

He looked into the room, eyed with interest the various bottles and tubes and burners on the tables, the piles of putty-like substance, of powders and pastes and coloring matter.

His eyes widened at a small, neat pile of semi-circular objects of various colors... objects that were shiny, glassy. He went forward slowly, stiff legged, reached out a hand.

"The eyes! The eyes!"

He saw at his right a heap of uncolored glasses of the same type. He grabbed one up. "My God," he said slowly. "How simple, and how clever! These are nothing but those new type eye-glasses… the things that you slip into the eye, under the lids. Contact lenses!—and colored to suit!"

With a wry grin at his failure to guess this when Slim had told him of the broken fragments in "Mason's" pockets, Satan pocketed the entire collection. He looked at the powders and pastes again, walked over and gently drew Marianne to her feet.

"It's very tough, kid," he said huskily. "Very tough to have happened at all, and infinitely worse for you to have to see. But—your father died in a very great cause, Marianne." He added softly: "And if he hadn't died, he might have lived to regret that he had ever been born."

Marianne leaned her head on his shoulder for a moment. "You're—you're *sure* that these are the criminals? And that you're—you're *not?*" she asked slowly.

Satan smiled gently. "What do you think?"

She nodded and blinked back her tears. "I believe you." She said simply.

Satan cocked his head suddenly. There were sounds, from somewhere in the front part of the house.

"What's that?"

Marianne listened a moment. "Oh, that? These men who are running this thing, the planning of 'doubles' for the President and the other important men—are keeping the doubles locked in this house until the time comes to use them."

Satan's brain raced along with the thing. After a moment: "But, why should they keep them prisoners?"

Marianne shrugged. "Maybe they can't trust them to stay out of sight until they are needed," she suggested.

"Maybe," Satan murmured. To himself, he thought: "And maybe these prisoners are the *real* people, the executives—while their doubles are now pushing this Maganni plot!" He whipped around.

"Does Coulter Kane have a double?" Satan asked. Marianne nodded.

"And who else?" he demanded.

"Senator Marra is the latest one they are impersonating," the girl said. "Senator Day Marra and the Secretaries of the War and the Navy. The head of the Treasury—that's about all I know of, now."

"Where are these people?"

"In a vault, in the front part of the house. They have provisions of food there, air vents and running water."

SATAN CONSIDERED. "Then, they could be left where they are for another twenty-four to forty-eight hours, without any danger of their health?"

"I don't see why not," Marianne said. "They've gone longer than that already, so—" She paused, her eyes widening with a sudden new fear.

There was a loud ringing of the bell upstairs. Satan froze in his tracks. Government men? Or some of the Maganni gang? But he knew that, either way, it would go bad with him.

He crossed the threshold and gently picked up the dead

Sarno; then he rolled the little gunman unceremoniously. He shut the door tight.

"Marianne," he said through tight lips. "We're in a spot—both of us! If that's some of this gang who have hoodwinked your father, they'll kill you as sure as you stand here. If it's Government agents?—you'll get life imprisonment, at least... *if* this set-up is what I think it is!"

"But—I've done nothing," Marianne protested, her eyes wide.

"You'll do something now," Satan told her with sudden decision. "I want a good sized sample of each of those pastes and powders your father makes. And throw the remainder down the sink! Get bags, or something, and take a lot of each!"

A pounding upstairs took the place of bell ringing. Satan pushed the girl gently to her task, then went through Sarno's pockets until he found a ring with two keys. He arose and located the rear steel door.

From upstairs there came the sound of a door crashing open. Satan turned to the girl.

"We'd better step, Marianne," he said softly. "Here comes the entertainment committee!"

The girl passed him the things she had gathered, then stooped quickly above her father. She kissed him gently on the forehead and wiped away the tears from her eyes.

"Poor dad," she murmured. "He was so *odd*, so wrapped up in his work all the time. He was almost a total stranger to me, except when he wanted to talk about his work. But he was gentle, Satan! He wouldn't harm a thing. And now, look—"

She was sobbing quietly when Satan unlocked the rear door

to the place and led her out. He turned and got a chair, then closed the door and locked it from the outside.

When he set the chair against the fence at the rear for Marianne to climb, he could hear the sounds of banging on the steel door to the laboratory... the laboratory where two dead men stood watch over the mysteries of the late Professor Sarno... mysteries that had died with the chemical genius.

Satan stopped in a shabby store in the grim neighborhood and telephoned Slim.

"I want the entire crew," he said. "They are to charter a plane and slam right down here. We're shooting the works to-night!"

"Right, Captain."

"Oh, and, Slim—don't bother to try contacting Frenchy. Frenchy has gone down the road." His eyes were grim when he added, "But not to join Mike! Frenchy has taken the other road—he's dead."

Slim's voice was exultant. "So he was the rat! I suspected him! You get him yourself?"

"I got him!" Satan said. "He's gone! Work fast, Slim. We are being hunted by both sides now. I just shot... Coulter Kane!"

"Oh, my God!" Slim gasped.

Satan said then, slowly: "At least, it was either Coulter Kane or his double!"

"His double?" Slim echoed. "But—?"

"I doubt if the President carries a gat," Satan said drily. "Or runs around without his bodyguards. But—Slim! I've hit on something definite, at last. There's a masked horde at work here in Washington."

"Ha!" Slim exclaimed. "And we're going to break them?"

"Break them, nothing," Satan laughed. "We're going to *join* them!"

CHAPTER 13
GENTLEMEN—BE SEATED!

MARIANNE WATCHED wide-eyed as the last of Satan's crew filed into the darkened room. Satan, sitting at her side, watched with keen eyes as the candlelight flickered over the men. Slim, behind him, stepped forward slightly when the last of the masked and robed men came through the door.

"All present, Captain," he said. "I've called the roll."

"Where's Frenchy?" Gentleman Dan's voice asked from behind a mask. His eyes suddenly halted on Marianne and a lazy smile broke across his mouth.

Satan saw; and glanced at Marianne. Gentleman Dan's voice was as attractive as that hidden face could be. Marianne seemed to feel its power.

"Miss Marianne Sarno—Gentleman Dan," he said. "Now, Dan? If we can get down to business…?"

"Sorry, Cap'n."

"Okay. Now, to answer your question—Frenchy made two mistakes: One—he joined the opposition and let me catch him. Two—" a hard note crept into his voice "—he was slow on the draw!" He spoke now to the mask that was Soapy's.

"I suspected you, for a time," he said. "When I make a mistake, I admit it." He turned to Slim: "Cancel Soapy's fines, add the same amount of bonus for him, to come out of my share. Soapy knew I had my ideas of him. Right?"

Soapy's mask grinned. "You had me on the hot spot, Cap'n."

Satan eyed each in turn to get his entire attention. "Now, men—listen carefully while I tell you what's up, what this game is all about."

Briefly but clearly, he outlined the happenings of the past few days, of his visit to the Atlas Bank, of Mason's amazing disappearance, of the Masked Horde in the house on N Street.

"And here's the plot," he continued. "Gold has already been transferred from the Treasury to the Atlas Bank. I'm positive that Maganni plans to get that gold. How? By planting doubles in important places in the Government, by having those doubles order certain shifts in their departments that will stagger the nation."

"I don't get it," Gentleman Dan said.

"All right," Satan elaborated. "Normally, a movement of gold from the country would attract plenty of attention. It might raise such hell that the transfer would be stopped. But—with the whole U.S. reading about other things that would stagger anyone's mind, who is going to bother worrying about a shipment of gold going out of the country?"

Gentleman Dan shook his head wonderingly. "In other words, Maganni is going to crack into the Treasury and do it legally. Is that it?"

"Right," Satan nodded. "At least, it will seem legal until it's too late to stop it. But we're going to beat him to it. We're going to stop him!"

129

"How?" came the terse question from behind Big Bill's mask.

"I am certain," Satan said slowly, "that those prisoners in N Street—that 'Masked Horde'—are not the doubles of prominent men. I suspect that they are the original, genuine, high officers of government themselves! I suspect that they are being held prisoners while this plot is being worked out to perfection!"

Marianne gasped. But Satan held up his hand for quiet. He went on: "I am so certain that I am going to make a little human collection of my own. I'm going to get those men and smash Maganni's game sky high!"

His eyes glowed as he scanned the circle of masked eyes. But there was only unbelieving silence that stared back at him. Satan nodded.

"Okay. I see you don't string along with me. What are the questions?"

Happy shrugged. "Look, Cap'n—why should Maganni keep those babies alive, those big men, when he can kill 'em off and save himself a lot of trouble and a lot of danger?"

The murmur of assent that came from the others was a challenge to Satan. He met it.

"Why should they be kept alive? First, if Maganni killed them, the search for their murderers would never halt; never! Two—with them alive and returned to their offices—after the financial crash that follows, after the national scandal that is sure to come—who would believe them? Can you imagine four or five officials saying, 'Oh, no. I didn't do these things. Sure; you thought you saw me, but that was really my double.' They'd be tossed out on their ears as the greatest liars of the age! The people's lack of faith in their own g o v e r n m e n t would lead to revolution!"

The masks were round-eyed as the appalling and cunning plot was clearly sketched for them.

"You're right, Cap'n," Big Bill acknowledged. "Me, I'd give it the horse laugh if I read that in the paper,"

"What nerve!" Gentleman Dan breathed.

"Right," Satan snapped. "And the only thing that will beat this plot is *more* nerve than they have. I could, I admit, unfold this plot to the officials now... anonymously, without their getting their hands on me. But I'm not going to for two reasons—

"First—The G-men will stay on my trail, even get me, maybe, unless I complete this job myself. Even then, they may not let up in their efforts to find out who I am. Besides, there's another angle that concerns all of us here... Maganni has a huge stake, a lot of money behind him. *I'm going to get it!* He owes it to me for my services, for attracting my attention!"

"What's next?" Gentleman Dan asked, obviously satisfied.

"Men—we're stepping into the hottest pot that's ever been

put to boil," Satan told them soberly. "If anyone wants to call it quits, let him do it now." His eyes ranged the group. "All in favor?"

"Aye!" Satan's crew boomed as one man.

"Good," Satan beamed. "Now—here's the plan: We've got pictures and color descriptions of some F.B.I. men. We've got some F.B.I. badges. And we've got the greatest make-up stuff ever devised, and an expert to help us put it on." He indicated Marianne, sitting at his side.

"We'll be F.B.I. operatives within the hour… calling on the key men that we want, strong-arming them over here. If I'm right?—we'll force Maganni's hand, panic him into a false move. If I'm wrong?" He opened his hands expressively.

"If I'm wrong, we'll be pulling the greatest boner in history."

"Silence!" he barked when a murmur of excitement ran through the group. "You, Soapy—to New York with you. Let yourself be seen in the—er—company from which I saved you several years ago!" Soapy shifted uneasily. "Keep your ears open, contact Slim if you hear anything."

"Right, Cap'n."

"Gentleman Dan," he said slowly, his eyes boring into the man, "I can't use you on this mission, either." Gentleman Dan's face fell. "I want you to help Miss Sarno with the make-up, then wait here with Slim as part of the reception committee."

Gentleman Dan grinned widely. "Tough luck," he murmured. Marianne blushed and looked away.

"Let's get started, Marianne," Satan said abruptly.

AN HOUR later, Soapy started wildly when 'Agent Jo Desher'

of the F.B.I. came out of the make-up room door. He blanched when the familiar features of "Tough Tom" Toomey of the same organization ranged up on his other side.

Satan's voice laughed out of Desher's mouth. "Where's your memory, Soapy? Desher is inches shorter, pounds heavier."

"Cripes, Cap'n," Soapy gurgled. His eyes bulged. "But if that ain't Tough Tom Toomey, I'll take a rap for life!"

"Says you," Big Bill's voice snapped in true Toomey style. Marianne and Gentleman Dan came out of the room.

"A perfect screen test," Satan-Desher grinned. "We fooled Soapy, and he ought to know!" His voice became businesslike. "All right, boys—you all know your assignments?"

"Right, Cap'n," they boomed.

"Happy hunting!"

GENERAL GARLOCK, Secretary of War, paced his big library nervously. An Army General Order lay on his desk, awaiting his signature.

General Garlock stopped before his desk, his eyes narrowed. In his mind he rehearsed the reasons for the shifting of Army Corps areas. The news men would be critical, alert, intelligent.

Again his mind came back to that terse phrase that had been spoken over the private wire of President Coulter Kane.... 'For the good of the Service.'...

Garlock's eyes lost a bit of their tightness, his short, powerful frame seemed to inflate with strength and determination. He dropped into the chair and plucked his fountain pen from its stand. Then the doorbell rang.

"F.B.I. men... Important..." he heard a voice say.

General Garlock looked into the mirror, then at the picture of himself on the desk. He smiled and poised the pen. He had started the first downstroke of signing 'David' as he called "Come in!"

A steely hand closed over his mouth and an arm strangled the breath in his throat. The pen was taken from his hand and snapped like a matchstick. He twisted madly, managed to turn his head slightly.

"Desher!" he gasped.

Then his orderly was in the room, fighting. 'Desher' dropped the man with a hard left hook, then clamped his grip tight again.

"For the good of the service," Garlock heard the words mockingly said, as he was dragged on his heels from the room.

JAMES HALDING, Secretary of the Navy, closed and locked the door when he heard Mrs. Halding enter the house. It had been reported around the Department that there had been scenes, of late….

He wondered, vaguely, why his manservant hadn't come for the orders, to carry them to the Navy Department. Signed and sealed, they lay on the mantlepiece of his library.

In another twenty-four hours, the combined Pacific and Atlantic fleets would be under a full head of steam with the Philippine Islands as a destination. In another week, at the most….

James Halding smiled archly… but the expression froze on his face when he heard footsteps hurrying up his stoop. The bell rang three times; imperiously.

He pursed his thin lips, felt his bushy white mustache, smoothed his hair into place.

"F.B.I.," he heard the cryptic announcement.

Halding half-rose from his chair, then dropped into it again. When the steps that mounted his staircase paused outside the door, he called pompously: "You may enter!"

He stared, then smiled slightly. "Ah, Desher! The light isn't so good, is—?" The greeting was broken off when he was jerked to his feet and had a gag forced into his mouth. His struggles couldn't stop Satan, disguised as 'Desher' from dragging him to the mantlepiece, couldn't prevent the ruthless destruction of those important orders in the fire.

Mrs. Halding was in the doorway. *"What are you doing?"*

"F.B.I., ma'am. And keep this quiet. One word about it and you'll be arrested, too!" An impressive badge was flashed.

"Oh!" Mrs. Halding glared at the Honorable James. "Keep him as long as you wish!"

"Good girl," 'Desher' chuckled.

"How dare you!" Mrs. Halding snapped.

"You'd be surprised how I dare!" 'Desher' grinned.

TREASURY SECRETARY Harold Pettiman glanced keenly at his visitor; then away.

"Well, Desher—those are orders. The President himself will confirm them to you, through your chief. That bank—" He paused, his head cocked. His eyes came around slowly.

"Do you hear anything strange? Some… noise? No? Well, Desher—we have secret information that this Satan person is set to block the gold shipment. We have precluded that. But—I want to warn you now: Should anything happen to that shipment, after it has reached the Atlas Bank, due—mind you—to your inability to get your hands on Satan—"

He stopped when the door of his office swung open slowly. A low, ominous voice asked: "Did you call Desher, Mr. Pettiman? I—Good God!"

Twin stared at twin, eyes incredulous. Pettiman gasped. Both Deshers went for their guns, but the taller one was the faster one.

"Up with 'em, Desher! Turn around! And so help me God, if you move I'll kill you. You, Pettiman—lie on the floor!" Mirth came into the strong voice. "That is, if you can summon the strength to move."

Desher was disarmed in an instant, his wrists pinioned with his own 'bracelets,' his coat draped over his shoulders. Pettiman was scorned.

"If you want to die, Pettiman—just squeak once. That goes for you, too, Desher," Satan added.

"Go to hell," Desher growled.

"That settles it!" Desher was gagged speedily and effectively. Satan whistled three times, softly.

"Okay, Cap'n," a low voice from the hall answered. "All clear!"

"Satan!" Pettiman choked.

'TOUGH TOM' TOOMEY turned to U.S. Senator Day Marra and said: "This way, Senator. He's out here."

Marra, political power and Presidential spokesman, boss of the Senate and champion of Coulter Kane's policies, blinked and looked around. His booming voice demanded: "Where is he?"

Tough Tom took one final look around the emptiness of the hotel corridor, then threw a punch from his heels. Marra went out cold. Tough Tom half carried and half dragged the man outside.

"Thank God I'm not a drinker," he said to the doorman meaningly, as he pushed the unconscious politician into the seat beside Kayo.

SATAN, STILL disguised as Desher, stepped into the room and surveyed the five prominent men gathered there—five men who were bound and gagged, with the exception of Harold Pettiman.

The Treasury Secretary sat limp in his chair, his mouth sagging.

"Come in, boys," Satan called over his shoulder. Then: "Masks for Slim, Gentleman Dan and Marianne. You—Kayo—stand guard."

Calmly, he walked from chair to chair, removing the gags. Senator Day Marra raised an uproar. Satan smiled pleasantly. "Go right ahead, Senator. Make out you're in the Senate chamber and gas all you want!"

Marra quieted and muttered threats, kept his eyes on 'Tough Tom.' After a minute, Satan silenced him with a growled, "Quiet, all! I want to tell you a few things that may be of interest to you!" When he had their attention, he went on:

"As you probably know, by now, I'm not Jo Desher." He pointed. "There sits Desher." He grinned mockingly "The best

The iron came closer the
fear-stricken face.

F.B.I. man in the game, even if he does hate work!" He sobered
suddenly. "I think all of you know how it is that I appear to be
Desher?"

He looked around, saw Pettiman glance at him quickly and
away again. General Garlock and Navy Secretary Halding
looked unimpressed. Day Marra growled, "I think you're a
lunatic." He stared at Desher and blinked. "One of you," he
added grumblingly.

"I'm smashing you!" Satan snapped suddenly, his face hard. "Smashing you like the rats you are…. Smashing you as I shall smash your boss—Joie Maganni!… when I get my hands on his filthy throat."

Desher started, his eyes round and his mouth forming an 'O.' Satan flashed him a look. "This was a pretty party that

Maganni staged… starting with the kidnaping of Banker Manse Mason and the substitution of his double. But Maganni knew it would work. He knew it—" he paused, his eyes on Jo Desher—"He knew it when King Cal Merrill was snatched on the eve of the World's Series and *his* double put into the game. Some bush leaguer who had gone sour, morally as well as physically, was able to stand out there and fool seventy thousand people. So why couldn't *you* fool the few that you came in contact with for a week or two?

"Maganni reasoned that if you can fool seventy thousand people, you can fool any number! But he overplayed his hand when he had emotionless, calm, placid King Cal throw a rage when he was yanked from the box!"

Senator Marra stirred. But he quieted again when Satan gave a steady look of warning. "That very day," Satan continued, "Manse Mason was snatched. And, in turn, each of the officials whom you men represent was snatched, you people taking their places! But the jig is up. The dance is over. And now you'll pay the fiddler."

He fixed each in turn with his eye, then said in a slow, hushed voice, "And I—Captain Satan—am the fiddler!"

He finished with Pettiman, and the Treasury official's face was ghastly when he looked away.

"I'm giving you five minutes, Pettiman or whatever you call yourself, to tell your story. Until then, until he is ready, the rest of you can relax." He turned to Slim:

"See if the gentlemen would like a little drink, Slim."

Day Marra growled, "I'd like a cigar. But I haven't one."

Slim made a sound of polite sympathy, leaned on Desher's shouldef as he made his way to the senator's chair. "Have a Corona, Senator," he said affably. He stuck the cigar half down the man's throat and held a match for him.

"I'll take one, too," Desher said. "I have one in my upper right hand coat pocket."

Slim inspected carefully. "No, you haven't." He stooped and peered at the man's neckband, putted his tie a bit aside. "By Jove, what a peculiar place to carry a cigar!"

Desher's eyes were groggy when Slim plucked the cigar and lighted it solicitously. "I must be going crazy," he muttered.

Slim nodded. "Wrong tense, Jo—you *are* crazy!"

Everybody started at the sharp report that came from one of the chairs. Day Marra's face was black with rage and ashes. The frazzled tip of his 'Corona' was smoking evidence as to where the explosion had taken place.

Slim said, "Dear, dear! What a noisy little boy!" He turned to Desher with a "Do you mind?"

He pulled the F.B.I. man's trouser cuff up a bit and inserted his hand into the top of the man's sock. When he arose he had another cigar. "Very kind of you," he said drily. But Marra didn't want it.

Smiling through his mask, Slim lighted the cigar himself and puffed contentedly. "Want a drink, any of you gentlemen?" he asked sweetly.

No one did, apparently.

Satan's voice was like a whiplash. "Time's up, Pettiman." He nodded to Slim. "Okay. The branding irons are hot, aren't they?"

Desher blinked; but maintained stolid silence. The War and Navy executives stirred uneasily. But Day Marra only laughed... harshly.

"You'll pay for your horse play, my man!" he boomed. "You'll pay."

Satan stared, puzzled. Slim halted in stride to turn. Senator Marra fixed both with a beady eye.

"The irons," Satan said again, shortly.

CHAPTER 14
MARKED FOR MURDER

WHILE HE was waiting, Satan turned to the masked girl.

"Get the solvent and melt off Pettiman's false face," he said. The official choked; but sat silent. Marianne was back in a matter of seconds with Gentleman Dan assisting.

The others sat spellbound as the operating began, at first under Pettiman's protest, until Gentleman Dan slammed his head back hard and held him straight in his chair with a throttling grip. Satan deftly flipped the false eyes out of those lids, then tossed them on the floor near the F.B.I. man.

Desher gaped, then blew the cigar from his lips with a choking sound when the stuff began to come off slowly. Deftly Marianne wielded a flat-bladed knife to remove a puttylike substance that rounded the man's weak chin, made the bridge of his nose suitably prominent. Water and more powder made dark, wavy hair out of what had been blond.

Satan called out: "Big Bill! Help Gentleman Dan with this stuff." He turned to Marianne. "You'd better go into another room and close the door."

"Oh." The girl stood irresolute a moment. "You're not going to—you won't—"

"The other room," Satan repeated grimly. "I'm working against time. Or maybe you'd rather watch?"

Marianne left as Slim came, holding two irons and an acetylene torch. Pettiman was jerked upright in his chair and three lengths of stout leather bound him tight. "Go ahead with the face washing, Slim is helping me," Satan said.

'Pettiman' whimpered. "Burn me all you want. I won't talk!"

"You'll burn and talk both," Satan snapped. "His head, Slim!" He grabbed an iron and held it to the flame, transferred it to 'Pettiman's' forehead with a quick movement.

There was a sudden sizzling sound. Pettiman the Pretender screamed and tried to throw his chair clear. But Satan held grimly while an odor of burning flesh rose in the room.

There was a sob from one of the other officials. Desher spoke up. "You rotten—"

"Cut it," Satan snapped. "I'm doing the talking." He turned. "How would *you* handle rats like this? Give them medals?" Desher fell silent.

"Talk," Satan snapped.

'Pettiman' sobbed aloud. "You rotten devil, I won't talk if—"

Satan plunged the iron back in the flames, this time pressed it to the man's right cheek. Another scream... and then, this time, a babbled:

"I'll talk! I'll talk!"

"You'd better not," Garlock growled from his chair.

Satan smiled harshly at Garlock. "You're next, for that!" To the broken gangster, "Spill it, and fast!"

"I—I'm in the Maganni fix," he gasped, his eyes crazed. "It was his idea; Maganni's. For a year, we've been coached, out in the West. Studied our parts, played them for him, later before acquaintances of the men we were to impersonate."

Satan said without turning, "Get this, Desher! You'll want to use it, later. Go on, Pettiman!"

"That's—that's all," the man attempted to stall.

"Oh, another iron?" Satan moved his hand.

"No," the impersonator screamed. "I'll tell the whole set-up. We made a gold transfer to New York, to the Atlas Bank. It got there to-day. Removal permits are signed and in Maganni's—"

"Maganni or Mesters?" Satan asked meaningly, his eyes shifting to Desher.

"They're the same man," the frantic mobster said. "Mesters is Maganni, fixed up. Just like us. Maganni has those permits, in case he has to highjack the bank to get the gold."

"Why would he have to do that?"

"In—in case something ruined the game. In case you, in some way, put a crimp on it by turning the Feds onto us."

"I'll finish it," Satan clipped. "Maganni counts on the publicity attendant on those Army and Navy removal orders to keep this hushed until he has the gold out of the country. Right?"

144

"You rotten devil!" Pettiman snarled. "You knew it, and yet you burned me to make me tell it to you again."

"Not tell *me*." Satan corrected mildly. "To tell Desher. And a rat like you ought to be burned. You're a menace to your country as well as to your community. You'd sell the United States out for any little grab you could get your hands on!"

He turned his head. "Kayo," he called into the next room. "Bring in the oil and bandages and wrap this mug up." He turned to Desher. "You get all that? You want it in writing?"

Desher was pale when he shook his head. "No. But I want you in irons, Satan!"

"Try and get me," Satan smiled as he moved to Garlock.

"Talk?" he said, his eyes hard.

GARLOCK NODDED. He opened his mouth to speak. But Satan suddenly held up his hand. "You're going to get burned anyway," he said. "Each one of you rats who was in this country-wrecking scheme is going to be tagged with my trademark so you'll be known to G-men and police all over."

Garlock swallowed hard. Satan looked at Gentleman Dan, who was working on 'Halding.' "How they've changed," he exclaimed. "I wonder what that stuffed shirt Marra will look like when you're through." He gave his attention to Garlock again. "Well?"

"I confess," the man said simply. "Maganni is the boss, Satan."

"Iron," Satan said briefly to Slim. He seized one of the man's arms, shoved his coat sleeve clear. Garlock gasped with pain as the hot device depicting Satan-with-pitchfork was pressed indelibly there. Halding was cleaned down by now, his face only remotely resembling the Navy Secretary he was impersonating.

"Anything to say?"

"Guilty," the man said sourly. "But Maganni is going to beat you, anyway. It's too late to stop him!"

Satan halted, turned at the hissed warning that came from 'Pettiman.' He walked back slowly. "You want some more?"

"No," the man whined. "I don't."

"You seem to know what this is all about," he said after a moment. "Suppose you squawk? You seem to have less guts than the others." He bent close. *"What does Halding, or whoever he is, mean?"*

'Pettiman' hung his head. "Maganni is blasting the Atlas vaults to-night," he said. "He was waiting to hear if the orders we were to pass along came through all right. If they didn't—he was going to move fast and blow with the gold."

Satan nodded. "So I have forced his hand! But he'll never get away with this."

Desher spoke from his chair. "They have treasury permits," he said slowly. "Okaying the removal if they were stopped after they had cracked the bank."

The 'phone tinkled in the silence that followed. Happy, from the doorway, called in, "It's Soapy. He wants to tell you something about a job he's got on tap."

Satan blinked. "Tell him I know what it is. Tell him to take it." He went back to Halding, compressing his lips. "It's got to be done," he growled. He pressed an imprint above the man's wrist. Kayo, following the brand, dressed each burn systematically.

Senator Day Marra was next. But there was something wrong. Gentleman Dan and Big Bill had been soaking and scrubbing and scraping the senatorial features without doing more than making them violently red. Satan stared.

"The hair. Soak the color out. Slip out the glass eyes." Satan ordered them.

Day Marra got the bath of his life; but his hair remained stubbornly what it was. He howled loudly when Gentleman Dan thrust a finger in his eye. Satan bit his lip. "I'm afraid," he said softly, "that we have made a mistake."

"You have," Marra roared. "You lunatic, you have!" He jumped

Slim

147

his head around at the snicker that came from Desher. "Sir? I'll see your chief about this!"

"So will I," Desher said sourly. "He bit like a sucker for this game and sent me around nursing these phonys. Anyway, Senator, it's the first time your neck has been clean in twenty years."

"Bah!" Marra snarled.

Satan stopped near Desher. "I haven't much time," he said slowly. "Any questions to be asked, before I dust out?"

"Yes," the F.B.I. man snapped. "Where are the officials these mugs are doubling for?"

"I left them in a house on N Street—right where I found them." He explained briefly. "You can find the President there, too, I believe."

"God!" Desher gasped. "They had the nerve to grab him?"

Satan nodded. "I had to shoot and wound one of the Presidents," he said soberly. "I hope it was the right one. I mean, the wrong one. So you see the spot I'm in."

"When do I get out of here?" Desher growled.

"I'm going after Maganni's bank roll," Satan said casually. "Don't worry—I won't touch even a bar of the gold. That'll be there... if I succeed. If I don't?"—he shrugged—"neither I nor the gold will ever cross your path again. If I get Maganni and his dough, I'll telephone your release. If I don't 'phone, you will be automatically let out in twenty-four hours."

Desher leaned forward and stared fixedly. "I think I know those eyes, Satan. I think I know those eyes!"

Satan stared back calmly. "Lucky you ever met up with 'em." He said as he turned away. Then he called, "Slim!"

"Yes, Captain?"

"I'm going into this raid as Mesters, or Maganni or whoever he is. Big Bill will go as Tough Tom Toomey. See if Desher can supply badges. We may need them."

"I've got only one," Desher growled, "I seem to lose that every time I sit down!"

But Slim was going through his pockets and had already produced three. Desher stared, his eyes unbelieving. "Tut, tut," Slim admonished him gently. "Holding out—holding out!"

"I never saw those before," Desher yelped. "What the hell is this?"

"Looks like a hock shop," Slim said, fishing another pair from the man's hair. He looked at them, then showed them to Desher. "These all seem to be the same number."

Desher made a choking sound. Satan turned his face away for a moment before he signaled Gentleman Dan. "I want you and Marianne to stick until I telephone," he said. Then, when his man looked disappointed: "I don't think you would want her to handle the job of turning these men loose, alone?"

"Hell, no." Gentleman Dan growled. "I want to handle *everything* for Marianne—from now on." He added a bit glumly, "That is, if she can ever forget you, Cap'n."

Satan's smile was a little sad. "You'll make her forget me or anyone else, Dan." He sighed. "She's a swell girl, Dan. But this job of mine is a solo job." He smiled more brightly. "Good luck to you both."

"Thanks, Cap'n," Gentleman Dan said huskily. "Now—the getaway routine, turning these men loose?"

"Simple," Satan said. "Just call F.B.I. headquarters. Tie these men well, don't take your eyes off them for a minute."

"Okay," Gentleman Dan nodded. "This is good-by, Cap'n?"

"It is. Make or break. You'll get your usual share in the usual way, from Slim. *If* we can get away with it."

He turned and left the room without a backward glance at the staring group.

SATAN GATHERED those of his men who were making the trip. "How's my make-up?" he asked.

The crew stared at the square-faced, dark man with brown eyes and shook their heads unbelievingly. "You're sure it's you, Cap'n?" Big Bill asked, drawing a general laugh.

"I feel fairly certain of it," Satan said drily. "Now, get this— We're on the last lap, boys. Maganni is blasting the Atlas vaults tonight. And we're going after Maganni and the dough he has there. Soapy is working on the job and won't know me. But I'll have to take my chances on that now. Tough Tom will get me by the cops—" he nodded at Big Bill.

"But from there, I'm on my own!"

"Maganni against Maganni," Slim breathed, showing great emotion for Slim. "It's magnificent, Captain! Magnificent!"

"Save the flowers," Satan said drily. "Wreaths may be in order before we're through."

But for all of their jocularity, there was a tenseness in the group as they left for the airport and New York. Satan was headed for the big round-up... a round-up that both he and his men knew stood more than an even chance of being his *last* round-up.

CHAPTER 15
PAYOFF IN LEAD

S ATAN AND Big Bill stood in the shadows of Trinity Churchyard and heard the bell toll one o'clock. Their eyes were on the side door of the great Atlas Bank, across Broadway and up one block.

Already they had seen nearly a dozen furtive figures slide along the building line and disappear into that side doorway. A uniformed patrolman walked slowly past them.

"Look!" Big Bill whispered. "Shall I slip out and steer him off?"

"Not unless you can digest lead," Satan murmured. "Don't you know that he's just a dummy, a plant? The regular copper on this beat is probably knocked as cold as an iced fish."

"Oh." Big Bill considered. "And—I suppose the Special inside the bank is a phony?"

"Either that or dead," Satan said grimly.

"It's some plant, all right," Big Bill said, his eyes wide. "Maganni makes this raid, gets the dough through with the Treasury permits, and ceases to be the suspected Mesters, simply by wiping that soup off his face! Pretty smooth."

Satan nodded grimly. "And we've got to be smoother to beat him." He cocked his head in a listening attitude. "I haven't heard a single one of the horn signals the boys were to give, when they drew up at their parking places."

Big Bill said, "Don't worry about them, Cap'n. You told 'em

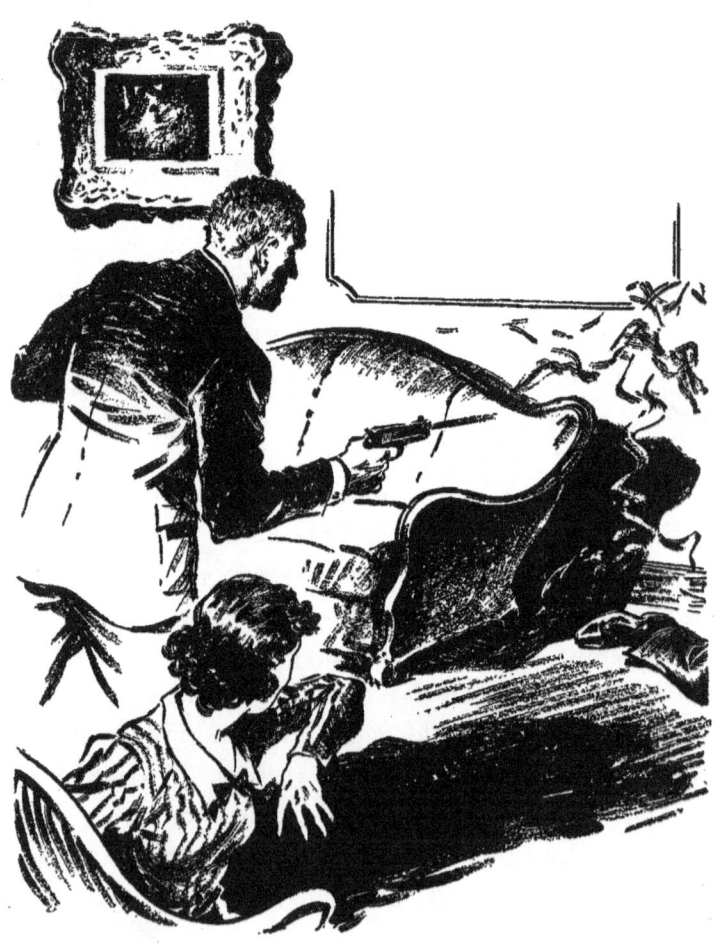

Satan returned the President's fire.

to park two blocks in either direction—all four of them—so

you could make whatever getaway you had to. They'll be there!"

"But I told them one o'clock sharp. And it's—" He stopped, his face breaking into a slight smile. From far away came the muted sound of an auto horn... three short, low blasts... then three more... and again three....

"There they are," Big Bill whispered.

Satan's face was tight. "We're sure to hear a slight cough, feel a rumble, at least, when that soup goes off in the vault. I've got to time this to get in right after that, because Maganni will work fast."

"You mean, Soapy will work fast," Big Bill grinned.

An elevated road train was coming up Church Street, rumbling heavily in the surrounding silence of the deserted financial district. Satan bent his head close to the ground. As the train roared by, he detected another rumble, felt the throbbing vibration. It was the explosive going off in the bank. The sound had nearly been muffled by the elevated train.

"Nearly missed it," Satan growled as he tugged at Big Bill's sleeve. "Maganni's not so dumb! Let's go, Bill! And remember—when I say 'Good night,' you go on down Broadway as fast as you can walk and climb into one of our cars. Don't mope around trying to look after me!"

"Okay, Cap'n," Big Bill said resignedly.

The two made the Wall Street corner, crossed the street and started up. They went at a leisurely pace, Satan waving his hands expansively as if explaining things to a tyro. He appeared not to notice the shadowy figures that flattened into the doorway up the street. But he stopped short of it.

"Everything's fine, Toomey," he said, with a laugh. "I'm just working late, as usual. You know bankers!" He laughed heartily again. "Well—you run along downtown and see about that little matter, will you?"

The replica of Tough Tom Toomey stood in full view under the street light. "I sure will, Mr. Mesters," he said clearly. "Thank you, sir." He turned and was gone, walking rapidly.

Satan stood in the light a long moment, then walked slowly over and stood opposite that doorway. His hand, thrust deep into the pocket of his gray coat, was gripped to his gun. But he forced his voice to be light.

"That was close," he said with a low laugh, addressing the doorway. "It's lucky I came out the other way and had a look around!"

A head appeared in the doorway. "Cripes," an amazed voice said. "It's—it's the Boss!"

Two more men appeared, as Satan walked slowly across and stopped. He stared into hard eyes that peered out from under low pulled hat brims.

"Sure it's me," he snapped. "Now, listen—keep your eyes peeled on that mug Toomey. He's a tough tomato. If he turns back, let him have it!"

"You bet," two of the men said. But another came close.

"I thought you were inside, Boss? How come you aren't? The soup just went off."

"Who the hell are you, that I should explain to you?" Satan was guessing that Maganni would handle such a situation in this manner. He laughed slightly then. "Can't blame me for being touchy, boys. But after tonight we'll be rich!"

His questioner mumbled an apology. And Satan stepped into the vestibule. He peered at the floor, saw something stacked along the wall. Machine guns… two of them. Carelessly, he picked one up.

"We'll need that more inside," he said, starting for the door.

He guessed that Maganni would have a key, guessed that the lock would have been changed since his daring raid that night from the Long Island hideout. If that door wasn't open—!

But it was. Satan waved a hand carelessly to the guards in the vestibule, then closed the door softly behind him. He stood with his back to it, as if getting his bearings like any other careful man. But he was sliding the door open slightly, setting the tumblers in the edge of the door so that it would lock automatically.

He knew that these guards—some of them, at any rate—would come into action as gold carriers, loaders, when the signal was given and the car brought up. An armored truck would probably be used, he reasoned.

No truck had been in sight when he came up, but he knew it could easily be in the delivery alley, behind the bank, ready for a signal. His eyes glanced through a dimly-lit window, saw the special officer walking nervously up and down. Then Satan slanted his eyes at the doors of the big steel vault in the dim light and felt a sudden clutch at his heart.

Slowly but surely, those doors were swinging open!

Satan counted ten, then stepped forward with a catlike tread.

TWO MEN were swinging the doors, a third squatted low, his beady eyes on them. That third man was Maganni. One of the others was Soapy, working hand in hand with the criminals. Satan grinned.

Slowly, Satan came close to them, the sub-machine gun he was carrying, held ready. But he stopped suddenly and slid behind a pillar. There were two more doors to be opened, he saw, when that first great pair had been swung.

Maganni rose from his squat and went forward fast. He slid a key into the smaller door, swung that. Then he unlocked the brass grilled door that was revealed. It was then that the special officer spotted Satan, and was coming over silently, his eyes narrowed.

Satan heard him and turned slightly. The man's eyes popped and started to swing to where Maganni was turning from the vault. Satan gestured suddenly, fiercely, to distract him. The ruse worked, drawing the wary guard's eyes back. He came nearer when Satan motioned and indicated that secrecy was necessary.

The special stopped two feet from Satan, his hand on his gun. And Satan swung with his tommy-gun, hard and accurately. But he couldn't stifle the loud groan of the man when he fell, nor the thud of his body.

At the sound, Maganni whirled... and the two men at the vault doors whirled with him. One, a huge, bull-necked man with the hard, broad face of a natural fighter, jumped for the machine gun that lay on a nearby desk. The other—Soapy—snatched an automatic from his pocket. But Satan held to his cover, not daring even to breathe.

For a moment he thought he would go undetected. And from where those three were, they couldn't see the special officer stretched out on the floor.

And then Maganni came forward slowly, his gat raised at ready.

Satan realized that his time had come… his, or Maganni's. And in the instant that it came to him, a plan fired through his brain. He had only one chance! And he had to work that perfectly. He waited until Maganni was only a foot from his hiding place. Then, his body still concealed by the immense marble pillar, Satan balanced the tommy-gun in his left hand while he slid his automatic out of his lapel holster.

Calmly and deliberately, he aimed at the three lights that were lighting the place. And with equal deliberation he shot them out, plunging the great banking floor into a roaring cavern of darkness.

Satan dropped to his knees and scuttled out from behind the pillar. And just in time. Maganni had spotted the line of fire, had leaped for the pillar with blazing gun. Satan rose into a crouch and fired again, twice.

Maganni cursed horribly, fell gasping to the floor. Satan jumped for the vault, jamming his automatic out of sight and snapping his flashlight into action. The rays were purposely slanted to let the light hit his own face, which the others would believe to be Maganni's.

But he hadn't reckoned on Soapy's smartness.

"That ain't Maganni," Soapy snarled, sensing some G-man

trap that he must break clear of. "Maganni didn't have no tommy-gun!" He fired as he yelled.

Satan dropped to the floor and crawled nearer to that partition of marble that separated them. He shouted hoarsely as he went, bending his entire efforts, his entire will, his entire strength, into making Soapy hear him. He had one chance only... Soapy's call letters... the emergency letters that were known only to Satan and his crew.

"Ess-Y!" He shouted. "Ess-Y. Ess-Y." Soapy's emergency call letters. They were all that would do it. If he were to shout "Soapy," the big machine gunner would probably kill Soapy, since he was no doubt known by another name among the mob members.

"Ess-Y!" Satan screamed again at the top of his lungs.

And then it happened.

Soapy got it; and yelled: *"Satan! Captain Satan!"*

There was a low moan from the big gunner and a moment later the dark was brightened by the orange streaks that stuttered from the mouth of his gun.

SATAN SLITHERED farther down the marble railing, came to his feet with the crazed gunner's lead still spraying the dark.

For one weird moment, Satan's flash lighted the mad scene... the gunner firing madly, Soapy crouched against the vault door... and on the door itself, throwing a shadow large as a giant, stood the silhouetted emblem of Satan with his pitchfork raised high.

The gunner whipped his fire crazily and poured it in a futile burst into that shadowy outline... poured it for two full seconds before Satan's own tommy-gun barked a rapid burst. The

Maganni gunner went down with a choking sob and pitched face first on the floor.

"Quick, Soapy! The doors. Swing them wide!"

Satan vaulted the rail and was at Soapy's side, and just in time knocked the gun aside. Soapy still didn't recognize him, was lifting his gat.

"Cut that, or I'll fine you that two thousand over again!"

"Cripes, Cap'n—! I couldn't figure your Maganni make-up!"

"Come on!"

Satan ripped the doors open, handed the tommy-gun to Soapy. "Stand guard while I get what we're after," he snapped. "Fire at anybody. *Anybody!*"

He stared at the immense pile of glittering bricks that stacked one wall of the place. High up the side they ranged, and along the entire length. He laughed lightly and went down the line of great drawers that lined the place.

There was a commotion in the outer bank now. But Satan's eyes were keened on the names that marked those drawers. The tommy-gun that Soapy manned stuttered suddenly, viciously, then stilled again. Satan flashed his light down slightly… stood, suddenly, with a smile creasing his features.

Louis Mesters, read the printed inscription on that metal drawer.

Satan tried it briefly, then drew his automatic. Calmly, he shot the lock off it, pulled the thing open. He smiled tightly at what he saw there. From the pocket of his jacket he jerked an ample canvas bag. He dished hand after hand of bank notes into the bag, until it was filled to the top. There was still one bill left in the drawer when Satan looked. He smiled grimly.

It was a one dollar bill! Satan said, "A dollar bill is plenty to leave that chiseler!"

Slowly, he shut the drawer, tightened the strings about the money bag, attached it to a button of his jacket. He snapped the flash off as he ranged alongside the still crouched Soapy.

"Follow me," he whispered. "Keep one hand on my shoulder."

From memory, he retraced his steps to the rail, slid over it, made his way to the opposite wall of the bank. Then he turned and felt his way down toward the side door. It seemed hours that he had been in the bank; yet Satan knew that it had been only a matter of minutes, minutes that were speeding and would bring after them a horde of police and G-men.

But suddenly he stopped again. A dark huddle was gathered near that exit. Motioning Soapy, with a push, to stay back, Satan called:

"Don't shoot, men. It's me—Joie Maganni!"

After a bated second, a voice growled back: "Show your light on your face if you're Maganni! But if you're not—!"

Satan flashed the light, holding a hand over it to kill the effect of the Satan figure that was pasted on that lamp. He stood immobile, knowing that he was under the most important scrutiny of his life.

"It's Maganni, all right," a voice said at last. Then: "Well? What the hell do we do now?"

"You scram," Satan snapped dousing the light suddenly. "Some rival mob is in on us. We shot it out with them and it's

"Yes, it's a very nice
night, Mr. Mason."

too late to grab the swag! We'll have the bulls in on us any
minute!"

"A rival mob?" one of the men started to question.

"Scram!" Satan screamed, flashing the light. The shadow flashed, just beyond the group.

"It's Satan! There he is now!" he shouted. To Soapy, he whispered: "Give 'em a few bursts, Soapy!"

"Wit' pleasure," the little man said and opened a wild burst of firing.

The remnants of Maganni's mob fled through the vestibule and up the street in wild disorder. Satan led the way to the door and out into the street. "Drop the Tommy," he said. "Follow me!"

Near the corner he stopped running long enough to emit three shrill blasts through his teeth. He breathed with relief when he heard a motor roar into high speed.

Kayo slid to the curb with hooded lights a moment later. Satan climbed in and pulled Soapy after him. As the car pulled away again, Satan murmured, "Well, boys—it's pay day!"

THEY DREW into a narrow street far down near the Battery. Uptown, the sirens of police cars screamed through the night.

Satan pulled down the shades of the big limousine and pulled three large bottles of water out of a side pocket. With Big Bill helping, he stopped looking like Mr. Louis Mesters. Soapy, his eyes wide, took it all in.

"I nearly got you, didn't I, Cap'n? Cripes!"

Satan laughed easily. "I haven't come much closer," he said.

Soapy stared some more. "Your hair's gettin' pretty long, Cap'n. I never seen it so long as—" He stopped. Satan's eyes were boring into the former safe cracksman.

"It doesn't pay to notice too much, Soapy," he said evenly.

Soapy dropped his eyes, then turned his attention out the window.

Satan dried his hands, adjusted his hat, stepped to the street. "I am going to telephone Washington now, boys. Gentleman Dan can release our prisoners—to Desher. And that reminds me." He pulled a paper from his pocket.

"How long will it take you to get to Bronx Park?"

Kayo blinked. "Twenty minutes will do it," he said.

"Good. I want you to get the rest of the boys and get up there right away, to carry out the orders you read there. Slim will take over that—er—payroll. You boys will meet him later for your share of the swag. The party is on that crook Maganni. This is good-by, men!"

"Good-by, Cap'n," they chorused. Satan shook the hand of each of them in turn.

"Good work," he complimented them. "And don't get stale." Then, before they pulled away: "Happy hunting, boys!" with a wide grin.

Kayo laughed loudly. "I ain't been to a zoo in years," he said.

CHAPTER 16
END OF THE HUNT

CARY ADAIR was at breakfast in his pine panelled dining room when the bell rang. He sipped his coffee and listened to Jeremy say:

"I can't say if Mr. Adair is in until I ask him, sir. You will have a seat, sir?"

Jeremy was very dignified, and his face was mildly disapproving. It was difficult being a 'gentleman's gentleman' properly when callers made their appearance so early in the morning, his attitude plainly said.

"Mr. Desher, sir, inquires if you are at home."

Adair pushed his chair back and threw his napkin to the table. "Jo, old man!" He walked with great strides into the living room and through to the foyer hall. "Jo, what a treat! Come in, come in! What a man you are. Y'know, I'm no more than back from my hunting trip then you pop in." He gestured to his silk pajamas and natty dressing robe.

"Excuse these, Jo—but we're not used to early company, Jeremy and I."

Desher followed him into the dining room slowly, then dropped into the seat opposite him. He nodded when Jeremy asked in a discouraging tone if he wouldn't have some coffee. But his eyes never left Adair.

"Where were you hunting, Cary?" he asked after a moment.

"Adirondacks; Canada. A bit more of it on the way back. Just a flying trip, you know. Pot one here, then off to another spot to pot another."

"Mind if I see what you got?" he asked slowly. "I'm sort of interested in hunting, myself."

Adair looked faintly worried, and a hard gleam came into Desher's eyes. "Jo?" Adair asked apologetically, "you won't let on, will you? I potted a deer out of season. And I managed to snare a couple of wolves and a small bear."

Desher's voice was deadly quiet. "Where are all these wonderful things you shot?"

Adair's expression changed to one of surprise. "Why, right here, of course." He raised his voice. "Jeremy! Jeremy!"

The servant entered and set a cup of coffee on the table at Desher's side.

Desher looked at Adair. His host obliged. "Jeremy—please show Mr. Desher the trophies of the hunt, while I have another bite of toast."

The F.B.I. man stood and followed Jeremy from the room. When he came back, he was wearing a baffled look. He dropped into his chair again, then sugared and creamed his coffee.

"You know, Cary," he said, a sheepish grin on his face, "I came to see you about—er—" He paused.

Adair leaned forward. "Money, old man? You want to make a touch? Don't hesitate, Jo. I have plenty."

Desher shook his head, turned when he heard Jeremy coughing violently. The servant bowed. "Excuse me, gentlemen." He disappeared into the pantry.

The radio was playing softly in the next room. Desher listened to the preamble of a new broadcast.

ADAIR CUT in on him suddenly. "Jo! About that man who was murdered on my roof—your operative, remember?"

Desher shook his head. "Mistaken identity," he said gruffly. "It wasn't one of my men after all. Turned out to be a gangster."

"Hm." Adair looked thoughtful. "Must have been a remarkable resemblance, eh? Tell me, now—how about all your crazy officials in Washington? You remember—?"

"Hush!" Desher hissed. "You shouldn't talk that way, Cary. What if someone heard you?"

"But, old man—!"

"I know," Desher growled. "I did say something of the sort. But—I was just over nervous, over tired. Everything is fine in Washington."

"Hm." Adair finished the last of his coffee and stood up. "I must invest in a few Government things. Was planning to until you said those things. By the way Jo—do you ever see the President? Coulter Kane?"

Desher stared at Adair steadily for a long minute. Then he nodded.

"Saw him just this morning—before I left Washington. He's—he's fit. Giving me a promotion, did I tell you?"

"Hello!" Adair exclaimed. "Now, that's something, isn't it. Any particular reason Jo? Big job you did?"

"No particular reason," Desher said slowly.

"Lucky dog!"

"*I'm* lucky?" Desher snorted. "What about you? Nothing to do but sit around and eat and talk and hunt and travel."

"I make money, too," Adair yawned.

"Yeah! What doing? Investing your money in oils, rails, utilities."

"Bank stocks, this time," Adair said negligently. He was suddenly alert, his ear cocked to the radio.

A strange occurrence at Bronx zoo last night, *the announcer was saying,* was the disappearance of some animals. The zoo was invaded by some pranksters who bound the watchmen and—

Jeremy was crossing the room swiftly, going toward the radio in the living room. He was at it, the instrument silent, when Desher walked into the big room.

"Turn that on again," he said brusquely. "I want to hear the rest of that!"

Jeremy seemed startled. "Did you think it was ours, too, sir? It must have come from another apartment, don't you think?" He raised the working lid of the machine, placed his hand inside. "Three bulbs, I think, are missing. At any rate, it doesn't operate."

He stood away. Desher looked at him closely, then peered into the thing. He blinked, clicked the contact button on once or twice, then listened intently. After two minutes he gave it up. "Funny," he muttered.

Adair shrugged. Desher signed to Jeremy to get his hat and coat.

At the door, Adair said, "Let me know when anything comes up again, like those crazy officials in Washin—"

"Hush!"

"Oh. I'm sorry. It's just that I'm always interested in what you're up to."

Jeremy stepped forward before he opened the door. "I think, sir, that this was an—er—a mistake?" He removed Adair's coffee spoon from the F.B.I. man's pocket.

Desher was dazed when he stepped into the hall and the

door closed on him. Adair smiled slightly and walked to the window overlooking the Bay. After a few minutes he turned.

"Jeremy! Have that deer butchered. The meat is to be hung for the usual time. Send the head to one of my clubs. Have the wolves dressed and send them to others of my clubs."

"The bear, sir?"

"Is it an unusual bear, Jeremy? A distinctive bear?"

"A very ordinary sort of bear, I would say, sir."

"Run-of-the-mill sort of bear, eh, Jeremy? Well—have it stuffed, complete; and send it to Mr. Desher. He might enjoy owning a thing like that. Poor fellow does so little hunting himself!"

Jeremy started away. But Adair wasn't quite through.

"And Jeremy!"

"Yes, sir?"

"Turn on that damned radio before you go."

"Very good, sir."

CARY ADAIR stared out the window again, the strains of soft music wafting across the room to him from his expensive radio. He stretched mightily, his fine shoulders standing hard under his lounging robe.

"Really, I should have a little excitement," he murmured.

POPULAR PUBLICATIONS
HERO PULPS

LOOK FOR MORE SOON!

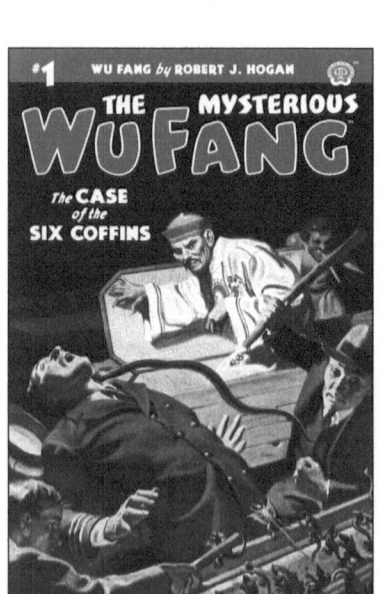

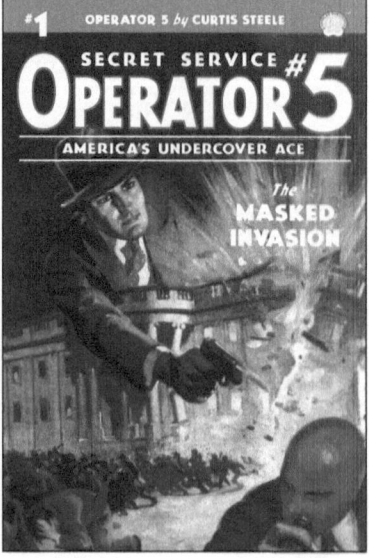

POPULAR HERO PULPS AVAILABLE NOW:

THE SPIDER
- ❏ #1: The Spider Strikes — $13.95
- ❏ #2: The Wheel of Death — $13.95
- ❏ #3: Wings of the Black Death — $13.95
- ❏ #4: City of Flaming Shadows — $13.95
- ❏ #5: Empire of Doom! — $13.95
- ❏ #6: Citadel of Hell — $13.95
- ❏ #7: The Serpent of Destruction — $13.95
- ❏ *NEW:* #8: The Mad Horde — $13.95

OPERATOR 5
- ❏ #1: The Masked Invasion — $13.95
- ❏ #2: The Invisible Empire — $13.95
- ❏ #3: The Yellow Scourge — $13.95
- ❏ #4: The Melting Death — $13.95

CAPTAIN SATAN
- ❏ *NEW:* #1: The Mask of the Damned — $13.95

THE MYSTERIOUS WU FANG
- ❏ #1: The Case of the Six Coffins — $12.95
- ❏ #2: The Case of the Scarlet Feather — $12.95
- ❏ #3: The Case of the Yellow Mask — $12.95
- ❏ #4: The Case of the Suicide Tomb — $12.95
- ❏ #5: The Case of the Green Death — $12.95
- ❏ #6: The Case of the Black Lotus — $12.95
- ❏ #7: The Case of the Hidden Scourge — $12.95

G-8 AND HIS BATTLE ACES
- ❏ #1: The Bat Staffel — $13.95

DUSTY AYRES AND HIS BATTLE BIRDS
- ❏ #1: Black Lightning! — $13.95
- ❏ #2: Crimson Doom — $13.95
- ❏ #3: The Purple Tornado — $13.95
- ❏ #4: The Screaming Eye — $13.95
- ❏ #5: The Green Thunderbolt — $13.95
- ❏ #6: The Red Destroyer — $13.95
- ❏ #7: The White Death — $13.95
- ❏ #8: The Black Avenger — $13.95
- ❏ #9: The Silver Typhoon — $13.95
- ❏ #10: The Troposphere F-S — $13.95
- ❏ #11: The Blue Cyclone — $13.95
- ❏ #12: The Tesla Raiders — $13.95

DR. YEN SIN
- ❏ #1: Mystery of the Dragon's Shadow — $12.95
- ❏ #2: Mystery of the Golden Skull — $12.95
- ❏ #3: Mystery of the Singing Mummies — $12.95

MAVERICKS
- ❏ #1: Five Against the Law — $12.95
- ❏ #2: Mesquite Manhunters — $12.95
- ❏ #3: Bait for the Lobo Pack — $12.95
- ❏ #4: Doc Grimson's Outlaw Posse — $12.95
- ❏ #5: Charlie Parr's Gunsmoke Cure — $12.95